She'd been kidnappe

A figure in fatigues leaped
her. A mask covered his fac
hand.

She ran. Rain fell fast and wild, obscuring her view.
The wind tossed her soaked hair. Bonds dug into her
wrists and sent pain shooting up her arms.

Her body smacked hard against the hood of a truck.

She gasped. The vehicle was nothing more than a gray
shape in the darkness and had seemed to come out of
nowhere. The driver's face was hidden in the darkness
and distorted by water pounding off the windshield.
She spun on her heels.

"Olivia!" a deep voice yelled. "This way."

She stumbled. A strong arm grabbed her around the
waist and nearly hoisted her feet off the ground. She
opened her mouth to scream. A hand clasped over
her mouth. "It's me, Daniel. It's okay. Just get in the
truck." He half steered and half pulled her toward the
passenger door.

Daniel? The complicated and moody man who'd told
her never to contact him again?

"Untie me. Now. And take me back to the diner."

"I can't. Sorry. Just get in. I'll explain when we're out
of here."

Maggie K. Black is an award-winning journalist and romantic suspense author with an insatiable love of traveling the world. She has lived in the American South, Europe and the Middle East. She now makes her home in Canada with her history teacher husband, their two beautiful girls and a small but mighty dog. Maggie enjoys connecting with her readers at maggiekblack.com.

Books by Maggie K. Black

Love Inspired Suspense

HEADLINE: MURDER

MAGGIE K. BLACK

HARLEQUIN® LOVE INSPIRED® SUSPENSE

Recycling programs
for this product may
not exist in your area.

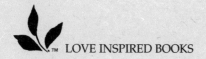 LOVE INSPIRED BOOKS

ISBN-13: 978-0-373-44683-4

Headline: Murder

Copyright © 2015 by Mags Storey

www.Harlequin.com

God will rescue me from these liars
who are so intent upon destroying me.
—Psalms 57:3

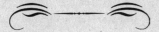

With thanks to all the amazing writers, editors
and others I've had the joy of sharing a newsroom with.
You all stretched and inspired me so much.

Most especially Doug, one of the best newshounds
I've ever had the privilege of working with.
Peace to you and Margie on your journey.

ONE

Shock rippled like a wave through the crowded Toronto courtroom, leaving a rumble of anger seething in its wake. The crown attorney had just announced that Brian Leslie, sleazy owner of Leslie Construction, was going to walk out the door a free man, despite stealing hundreds of thousands from both the government and his own employees. Which meant the construction crew he'd left both unemployed and broke had just seen their best hope for justice go up in flames.

Reporter Olivia Brant tightened the grip on her notepad. Her green eyes grew wide. That man's sloppy, reckless attempts at tax evasion had made headlines across Canada. How could the authorities possibly think it was "in the public interest" to let a thieving creep like him go free? Growing up, always shuffling from one lousy rented apartment to the next, she'd seen all too well how working for really bad bosses could tear someone's family apart.

Well, even if I don't succeed in saving my own position at Torchlight News, *at least the last story I write will be about something I care about.* Although hopefully, if she acted fast enough, this would turn out to be the one big news story that actually kept her from losing her job.

Olivia tightened the clasp holding back her fiery red mane and leaped to her feet. The camera that she'd nabbed off a coworker's desk clattered to the floor. She scooped it back up and pushed through the rows. The courtroom was packed to the seams with former Leslie employees eager to see Brian pay. Now that justice wasn't coming, the room felt like a mob waiting to surge. A large bald man with a hawk tattoo on his neck cursed and gripped the seat in front of him until his knuckles cracked. Beside him, a woman with spiky hair cried loudly.

Brian sat alone and was grinning so widely he might as well be gloating. The only other living member of the wealthy Leslie family was Brian's teenage niece, Sarah. Much to the media's dismay, the seventeen-year-old heiress hadn't agreed to any interviews about her uncle's arrest and hadn't attended his trial. Didn't look as though any friends had shown up to offer Brian support, either. Olivia wondered if the rumors of his gambling addiction and drug use were true.

Any moment now, he'd walk out of the courtroom, head down to the private parking garage and drive out as a free man into the hot summer air.

When he got to his vehicle, she'd be waiting.

Dear God, please help me get this interview with Brian Leslie. Or at the very least a picture and a quote to make my article solid enough for the front cover. I really don't want to lose my job. The newspaper's the only place I've ever really felt at home.

Prayer slipped through her heart like an instinct. It was funny, no matter how many times she tried to put her childhood faith out of her mind, whenever stress hit she could feel it pushing back in at the edges. Not that all the desperate prayers she'd prayed as a child had ever kept her dad from losing one job after another. While Vince, her editor at *Torchlight News*, was one of the most dedicated people of faith she knew, that still didn't alter the fact that recent changes at the paper meant he was going to have to lay off almost a third of the staff by September.

Her phone buzzed with a text message. It was from Ricky, a young photographer at *Torchlight* who was probably facing the chopping block, too.

Hurry back! Vince is looking for you. Also, you seen the camera? R.

Guilt dripped down her conscience like a nagging cough she couldn't clear. She hadn't told Vince she was covering the Leslie Construction trial. There were dozens of potential stories like this in Toronto every day. *Torchlight* could only afford to send reporters out to so many. Newspaper policy was that writers brought their article ideas to the weekly story meeting, like treasure hunters piling their maps into the middle of the table. Vince would then decide which stories would get reported on and who covered what. Getting a good, hard crime story meant a chance at seeing your story hitting the front cover. He'd never given her that chance.

Maybe Vince won't like that I just took the initiative and jumped on this story without asking. But if I pull it off, it'll prove I have what it takes and he'll think twice about letting me go. Or at least, it'll give me a great story on my resume to help with my job search.

Her fingers slid over the handle to the stairwell door.

"Hey! Where do you think you're going?" A large hand landed on the door in front of her. She turned, coming face-to-face with a young man in a dark blue police uniform and a bushy blond beard.

"I'm sorry. I was just—"

"You can't go down there."

Olivia rolled her slender shoulders back and stood tall. Sure, she was only five foot two, and this man was easily twice her size. But she'd worked in a newsroom long enough to know police couldn't just block public access somewhere without cause. This belligerent officer hadn't even flashed her a badge.

She flashed him her media credentials. "I'm a journalist with *Torchlight News* and, yes, I can. This is a public stairwell and you have no legal reason to detain me." His eyes narrowed. In her experience, while most cops were amazing, a handful of them got just a little too used to throwing their weight around and expecting the public to obey. Not the type of cop a reporter ever wanted to tangle with. What was worse was this cop had even covered the badge number on his uniform, so she wouldn't be able to report him—an illegal but sadly not unheard-of practice that the chief of police had been clamping down on hard. She raised the camera, hoping the thought of being caught on film would be enough to make him back down. He just scowled.

"Is there something else going on here that I should be reporting on?" she asked.

A loud crash came from behind them, along with a whole lot of yelling. She turned. A muscular dark-haired man was being forcibly ejected from the waiting area. He was putting up such a fight it took multiple guards to handle him. The blond officer snickered.

Olivia ducked under his arm and dashed down the stairs.

"Hey!" The questionable cop's voice bellowed through the staircase like a freight train. "Stop!"

Her feet pelted down one flight of stairs. Stopping wasn't an option. But maybe a route change wasn't a bad idea. She hit the second floor, slipped through a side door and came out on an administration level. Her footsteps sped up, weaving through rows of people waiting for their trials to be called. She went down one more staircase and came out on the opposite side of the parking garage. The officer was gone. A slight smile crossed her lips.

The garage was dark, lit only by the eerie glow of yellow fluorescent lights. She readied the camera. The state-of-the-art equipment would just keep snapping once she pushed the button, taking hundreds of pictures a minute. She only needed one of the pictures to be usable, so the odds were in her favor. Brian's car was to her right.

That was when she noticed the truck. The bright green pickup was parked a few spots away, looking like a flash of sunlight on a fresh spring leaf compared to the sea of concrete around it. Her breath caught. There was a man in the driver's seat. He was tall and rugged, with broad shoulders and a faded plaid shirt. Strong arms rested on the steering wheel. His head was bowed, showing a mop of chestnut-brown hair that curled slightly at the neck. He looked nothing like a lawyer. Bit too casual for a journalist, at least from anywhere reputable. A member of Leslie Construction's crew, perhaps? But then, why would he be down here instead of in the courtroom?

He glanced her way. His eyebrows rose. She looked down at her camera.

The door to the staircase flew open. Her camera started snapping. Brian Leslie walked through. He glanced around the garage, turned back toward the stairs for a moment, then hurried to his car.

"Mr. Leslie!" Olivia started across the parking garage toward him. "Olivia Brant, *Torchlight News*. What do you have to say to your former employees? Are they ever going to see the money you owe them?"

"Seriously?" He laughed and yanked his car keys from his pocket. "You heard how those ungrateful jerks booed me in court today? As if my family didn't keep them working for years. You tell them that I'll be dead and buried before they get one more cent of money from the Leslie family. Tell them fat chance winning in civil court now." He pressed the button on his key fob to unlock his car. The car didn't respond. He frowned and jammed his finger on the button. Nothing happened. "Stupid waste-of-money car."

Then, it was like everything happened at once.

A stairwell door banged open to her right.

Three figures in black fatigues and blank featureless masks ran toward Brian.

Three men without faces.

A gunshot split the air. Olivia screamed.

Brian wheeled around. Blood spread across his chest.

His car exploded in flames.

* * *

Daniel Ash froze with his hands on the steering wheel. The scene unfolded in front of him through a haze of smoke and fire. Just moments ago, he'd been sitting there trying to pray for Brian Leslie—an endlessly unpleasant man who he'd briefly called his brother-in-law a very long time ago.

Then Brian walked into the garage, three masked men surged from the shadows and the world erupted in fire.

A car bomb. A weapon fired. A bullet through Brian's chest.

It was like Baghdad, Manila and Damascus all over again.

Here. In Toronto.

Just moments ago he'd seen a woman running toward Brian. Now her screams echoed through the flames.

Instinctively, Daniel yanked open the glove compartment to feel for his bullets and gun. It might be too late for Brian. But he could still save the beautiful stranger from the line of fire.

His hand came up empty. There were no bullets. He had no gun.

Reality hit—Daniel wasn't a bodyguard anymore. His handgun was long gone.

He was just a regular guy back home in Canada, a place where it was incredibly difficult for a personal bodyguard to even get a license to carry a handgun. This wasn't his first firefight. But this time he was unarmed and unprotected, without even an armored vehicle to shield him.

His hand gripped the door handle. His eyes rose in a split second of prayer.

Lord? What do You want me doing right now? Can I still save her?

More gunfire now. Sounded as though only one of the masked men was firing. But he couldn't see either the shooter or the target, just a series of bangs and flashes in the billowing smoke.

The woman's screams fell silent.

He'd never once run from danger. But like it or not, his hero days were over. Daniel had given up being a bodyguard four years ago, because his former step-daughter had no one else to turn to. *I made a commitment to be Sarah's legal guardian.* With her uncle Brian's death, the teenager was now the last remaining member of the Leslie clan. For all he knew, whoever had killed Brian would now be coming after her, too. He needed to be there for her. He needed to protect her.

How can I risk my life to save a stranger? The woman might not even still be alive.

Reluctantly, Daniel turned the engine over. He grabbed the gearshift, ready to drive. Then, through the smoke, he saw a flash of red hair. She was running toward him, beautiful and terrified, like a phoenix rising. Dark lashes fringed eyes wide with fear. Auburn hair tumbled loose around her face.

He couldn't just leave her to die.

Daniel threw the door open. "Here! This way! Run to me—"

A second explosion shook the air and tossed her onto the ground. Daniel leaped from the truck. He pelted across the parking garage—toward the flames, the chaos and the woman now lying still on the con-

crete. In moments, Daniel had reached her side. Her
eyes were closed. But when he clasped her wrist, he
felt that her pulse was strong. He scooped her up into
his arms—bag, camera and all—and cradled her up
against his chest. He ran for the truck. A huge, faceless
brute of a man loomed out of the smoke and yelled at
Daniel to stop. He kept running. Bullets ricocheted in
the darkness behind him. Prayers poured from his heart
over his lips, "Please, God, guide me now!"

He climbed into the driver's seat, not letting his
strong arms loosen their grip on the woman's body for
an instant. As he slid her off his lap and into the passenger seat, her press pass caught his eye—Olivia Brant,
Torchlight News. He reached across to buckle her seat
belt. Her cheek brushed his shoulder. Luminous green
eyes fluttered open, inches away from his own.

"Olivia? Hey, my name's Daniel. Don't worry. It's
going to be okay. You're safe here with me." He glanced
up and counted three masked, black-clad figures in the
haze. The brutish one now had a gun in each hand. A
short man was fiddling with a small box. An extremely
thin one barked orders at them both. The big one raised
both guns toward the truck. "And we're getting out of
here." Daniel slammed his door. "Right now."

He hit the gas and swerved a hard left, narrowly
steering the truck between the thin man and a concrete support pillar.

"Daniel?" Her voice beside him was faint. "Who
are you? What are you?"

Thank You, God! She was both conscious and able
to talk, which hopefully meant no serious injuries, even
though her mind was probably reeling and her ears
would be ringing. No doubt she wanted to know what

kind of man had just scooped her into his truck. But now was no time for long answers. The short version would have to do.

"I used to be a bodyguard." He focused his eyes on finding an exit. "Spent a decade overseas. War zones and danger spots mostly. Getting someone safely from point A to point B like this was kind of my specialty. Now I'm just a carpenter." One who apparently could still swerve around an obstacle course of parked cars and concrete at full speed.

"Carpenter?"

He couldn't tell if that was really a question or if she was just repeating back the only word she'd managed to catch. Depending on how hard she'd hit her head, she might not even remember any of this. "How are you feeling? There's a hospital only a few blocks from here. That's where I'm taking you. If you've a phone handy, please call 9-1-1. We've got to let the police know what happened here."

He couldn't begin to guess how much of the garage was actually covered by security cameras or how security would respond to whatever they saw. Sometimes surveillance only covered the stairwells and exits. For all he knew, they'd just seen smoke and were treating it like a car fire. Instead of…what exactly? A terrorist attack? *Some kind of organized crime hit on my former brother-in-law?*

There was no answer from Olivia. Daniel risked a sideways glance. Her eyes had closed again. There was a cell phone in his jacket, but that was in the backseat and he wasn't in any position to reach it. Could he afford to stop, grab his phone and call the police before he reached the hospital? No. He had one task right

now and one task only—saving the life of the person
in his care.

"Thank You, God, that we're both still alive," he
prayed aloud. "Please have mercy on everyone else
who might be in danger. Please prompt someone else to
alert the authorities. Any help and guidance You want
to give me right now would be awesome."

An engine roared behind him. The sound echoed
off the concrete walls. There was the crack of a gun
being fired and the clang of a bullet hitting his tailgate.

He raced up the final ramp. Another shot was fired.

His truck's rear window exploded in a spray of
glass.

TWO

Glass hit the back of Daniel's seat and fell down around them like rain. He clenched his jaw, pressed the gas pedal to the floor and forced his mind to block out everything but the growing space of sunlight ahead. The ticket barrier was unmanned, and he wasn't about to stop at the machines to pay for parking. He just had to hope some security guard somewhere had seen this all go down on a monitor and called the police.

He swerved around the barrier and clipped the edge of the wood. Then he was outside, blinking in the bright summer sun. Smoke poured through the tunnel behind him. A few passersby were stopping to film it on their phones. A couple more took pictures of his broken back window as he merged into heavy downtown traffic. Hopefully someone had the sense to call 9-1-1. Another murmur slipped through Olivia's lips. Delicate color had returned to her cheeks. Sunlight filtered through the window, setting her hair alight in a cascade of red and gold.

Tires screeched behind him. His gaze shot back to the rearview mirror. A black van with tinted windows shot out of the parking garage and forced its way into traffic. It was five car lengths back. No one was firing now, but the van whipped back and forth between lanes as the driver fought his way closer.

The gunmen were following.

Emergency vehicles streamed toward him on the opposite side of the street. That was one prayer answered—someone had called the authorities. But would they head straight to the garage, or would anyone notice his predicament? He flashed his lights, honked his horn and waved a hand out the window in the hopes of grabbing an officer's attention. The cops flew past. Apparently a broken back window hadn't been enough to raise suspicion. And he wasn't about to stop.

The gunmen were now only two car lengths behind. He cut through a parking lot, swerved into an alley and came out on another street. The van followed. He could see the driver now. It was the tall one of the three. He'd pulled a hood over his head to keep the mask covering his face from drawing the attention of anyone not looking straight on. But Daniel could still see the mask—black, oval-like fencing gear and utterly featureless. Would they be brazen enough to open fire on a busy Toronto street? The light ahead of him turned yellow. Daniel gunned the engine and flew through. He hit the other side of the intersection seconds before it turned red. The van followed tight on his tail. The vehicle was now so close he could practically feel it tapping his bumper.

The hospital sign appeared ahead. Cars lined up to enter the hospital parking lot, but Daniel wasn't about to wait. He aimed straight for the emergency-vehicles ramp. Two cop cars and an ambulance sat near the emergency room door. He hit the brakes beside them.

A smattering of hospital staff and police ran toward him.

The black van kept going, disappearing into traffic.

"Hey! You can't park here!" A paramedic reached him first. "You have to go around to the lot—"

Daniel threw the truck into Park and leaped out. Shards fell from his clothes. "This woman needs help and might have a head trauma. There was a car bomb inside the courthouse parking lot. People shot at us. A man named Brian Leslie was just murdered. Wait—be careful. The truck is full of broken glass."

Two paramedics eased Olivia out of the truck and onto a stretcher. Daniel turned to follow her. A hand tapped his shoulder.

"Sir, you'd better follow me." It was a hospital security guard, flanked by a uniformed police officer.

"Absolutely. I want to give a statement. Just let me get her stuff first." He turned back to the truck. The messenger bag had spilled all over the floor. He scooped the contents up quickly. Her press photo identification badge was hooked on the edge of the seat. He pulled it loose, allowing his eyes one moment to linger over the adventurous curve of her smile. "Her name is Olivia Brant. She's a newspaper reporter."

The security guard took her belongings from him. "What's your connection to her?"

I'm her bodyguard.

The answer he'd have given in his former life flew through his brain automatically and he just barely caught himself before it left his mouth. "Absolutely none. I just happened to be there when the bomb exploded and saw she needed help." His eyes glanced toward the emergency room door. He couldn't see where she'd gone. "But if it's all the same to you, I'd like to stay and give my statement here. Just in case she needs anything. Or at least stay until you're able to reach her emergency medical contact, so she's not alone."

He had no real reason to stay. Yet something inside was urging him not to go.

"Sir?" The officer's tone was definitely a little sharper now. He took another step toward Daniel. "I think you'd better come with me."

Words swam in a jumble of black-and-white on Olivia's computer screen. A pencil spun between her fingers. It had been two days since Brian Leslie had been murdered and her memory of the event was still nothing but an incoherent mess of disjointed images. She leaned back in her chair and listened to the clack of her colleagues' fingers hitting keyboards. It was Friday afternoon and she seemed to be the only one blinking bleary-eyed at a story that wouldn't come together. She added a few more pencil lines to the sketch in her small pocket-size notebook.

A blank oval face, like a black fencing mask, stared back at her through a haze of charcoal smoke swirls.

"Hey, can I borrow that a second?" Ricky rolled his office chair across the alcove from his desk to hers. "I want to check it against something I saw online."

"Help yourself." She shrugged. "It's all I can remember of the killers. But it's not much to go on."

The young photographer picked up the notepad and rolled back to his computer. "I never knew you could sketch like this. Why aren't you in the graphics department?"

She shrugged. "I really enjoy writing." *And editing,*

graphic design, ad layout and photography. Over the past few years she'd settled into a pretty comfortable role at the newspaper as a "bit of everything" journalist who could write one day, edit the next and field a decent classified ad page in between. But being good at a little bit of everything wasn't the same as proving to Vince that she belonged on his new, smaller team.

Last summer, Vince had gotten into a major battle of wills with *Torchlight*'s former publisher when they'd tried to force him to fire crime reporter Jack Brooks over his investigation into the Raincoat Killer. So Vince had bought out the newspaper and turned it into a scrappy independent. Which was actually awesome, except that he'd warned them it would mean cutting staff. Now was no time to have a mind full of smoke and haze.

Her temples ached. If she closed her eyes, she could almost recapture the memory of the man who'd saved her—dark eyes, a voice as deep and soothing as a morning cup of coffee, chestnut hair curling ever so slightly at the nape of his neck. *Daniel.* But then she'd blink and he'd be gone again.

"Hey, Olivia? Come look at this."

She slid her chair over. It was an internet web page. Three crude figures in black fatigues and featureless fencing-style masks stood in the center of the screen under the words *The Faceless Crew.*

The sudden reminder of how terrified she'd been sent adrenaline coursing through her. "What is this?"

"It's a fragment of a website that was shut down a few weeks ago." Ricky ran one hand through his shaggy hair. "Remember that car bombing in Vancouver last June that turned out to be some turf war between small-scale rival gangs? These guys tried to take responsibility for it and a few other car fires, too. They posted some stuff on various hate websites, trying to get attention as some kind of homegrown terrorist group for hire. No one took them seriously."

She vaguely remembered Ricky bringing it up at a news meeting weeks ago. Vince had said no hard facts equaled no story and that the paper wasn't in the business of chasing ghosts. But it seemed these men weren't ghosts anymore. "Can you print it for me?"

"Yup, and look here." He zoomed in. "I was able to recover some text, too."

She read out loud, "'The Faceless Crew are a gang of three killers. Rake is the strategist and leader. Brute is the weapons expert and, ah…assassin. Shorty is the explosives expert.'" She looked up. "They misspelled *assassin*. Looks to me like three brash, delusional kids who watched too many action films and decided to go start their own gang."

"You can see why no one took them seriously."

Right up until the moment they planted a bomb in the court garage and killed a man. Then again, an alarming number of gang-related murders, and even terrorist attacks, were committed by angry, mentally unstable young men whom no one took seriously at first.

They walked over to the shared printer and waited for the page to come through.

"Is it possible someone got them to murder Brian Leslie?" Ricky asked.

"I don't know." She ran both hands through her hair, then twisted it into a knot at the back of her neck. "Brian owed his crew a lot of money. They hadn't been paid in weeks. He'd skimmed money off their checks. He had them working off the books without them knowing it, which meant they can't even claim unemployment now. So I can imagine a lot of people wanted to hurt him. But there are far easier ways to get justice than hire contract killers with gang ties."

The paper inched its way out of the printer. "What happens to the company now that he's dead?"

"It's a family business, started by Brian's father. The only remaining member of the Leslie family is Brian's niece, Sarah. But she's just a teenager and can't inherit anything until she turns eighteen sometime this fall." It was any guess how she'd handle the mess her uncle left behind. "I'm just sorry I lost the camera. If I still had it, we'd have photographic proof that these were the guys. But it wasn't in my bag at the hospital, so I can only guess it's now buried in rubble. You want to come with me to talk to Vince?"

Ricky shook his head. "No. Just try to talk him into keeping me on staff if this turns into something."

Torchlight's editorial pool shared the large top floor of a converted Toronto townhouse. She climbed down the steep stairs to the second floor, went down the hall and knocked twice on the editor's door.

"Come in." Somehow Vince's salt-and-pepper hair seemed even grayer than usual. His tweed jacket was pushed up over his elbows. She laid the printout on his desk. He leaned on his desk with both hands and stared down at it. "What am I looking at?"

"Something Ricky found online." She took a deep breath. "I think this might be who I saw kill Brian Leslie."

"I seem to remember Ricky showing me this printout before." Blue eyes glanced up under bushy eyebrows. "You already know what I'm going to say about it, don't you?"

Yup. Theories were for the writers' meetings. Facts were what got printed in the paper.

"I know we can't just print that these three random men might have been involved in this murder without something solid behind it." Reporter Thinks She Kind of Remembers Seeing Three Masked Men Who Could Be the So-Called Faceless Crew was hardly a headline she'd put on the cover of the paper, either. "But I'll get something solid. I've put in calls to the police, Sarah Leslie and the crown attorney's office. I'm just waiting for someone to call me back."

Not to mention, she'd also tried calling her older sister. Chloe was a detective in Northern Ontario. While this was hardly her jurisdiction, her sister had an incredibly practical way of looking at things that Olivia found both infuriating and helpful. Besides, it was always wonderful to hear her voice. But Chloe hadn't called her back, either.

"Well, I've never seen police and the courts put such a tight lid on a story." Vince sighed like an ancient freight train billowing steam. "And every news outlet in the country will be after an interview with Sarah."

"Yes, but not every news outlet has a reporter who was there in the garage when her uncle died."

"Oh, you don't need to remind me." A reluctant half smile crossed the newshound's lips. "You should probably be thankful I didn't fire you over that."

A flush rose to her cheeks.

"Any progress tracking down the other witness?" he asked.

"Daniel? No, but I'm pretty sure he said something about being a carpenter." And also a *bodyguard*. Her memories of him were so larger-than-life it was hard to know if they were all real. "But his truck was pretty distinctive. I thought that if I went around visiting some construction sites, I might find someone who knows who he is."

"From now on, I want you to limit your pursuit of this story to email and telephone." Vince crossed his arms. "This whole Faceless thing looks more like urban legend than fact, but anyone capable of murdering a man and blowing up his car inside a government building is more than capable of taking out a lone reporter. We can all sit down as a writing team next week, talk it through together and decide how to proceed. There might be other tacks we can take on this."

Her heart sank. "You mean, there might be other reporters you could put on this story."

"We're a family here, Olivia." Vince frowned. "You know that. As an editor, it's my prerogative to assign stories however I think will serve the paper best. Jack is our crime reporter. He's got expertise in things like this. True, he's off on a book tour right now, but he'll still be able to take lead on this one remotely."

She looked down at the ground. Just because Vince liked to say the staff were family didn't mean it was accurate. Everyone was loyal to the paper, but it wasn't the *only* loyalty everyone had. Jack had his book tour. Their sports reporter Luke was working freelance from new digs up north after having reconnected with his former sweetheart. Everyone was keeping an eye out for other opportunities to pay the bills. She came to work every day expecting to be told to pack her metaphorical suitcase. What good was a family if some people just left to chase their own dreams—and others were kicked out?

Her cell phone started to ring. She glanced at the number but didn't recognize it.

"I'll let you get that." Vince leaned back. Worry filled his gaze. "Monday, I want you and I to sit down and talk through your future with the paper. I'm sorry, I know you really want to move to writing full-time. I'm just not sure that's where your talents are best suited."

"Got it. Thanks." She nodded numbly.

How on earth am I going to change his mind over the course of a weekend?

She went out into the hall and closed the editor's door behind her. Thankfully, the caller hadn't given up. "Hello?"

"Hello, Olivia?" The voice was deep and soothing, yet somehow it still managed to send shivers running down her spine. "This is Daniel Ash, the man from the parking garage."

Her breath caught in her chest. Daniel?

For a moment, she nearly ran back into Vince's office to put the call on speakerphone.

If only he hadn't just said he was thinking of assigning the story to someone else and that she didn't belong in the writing pool.

"Daniel! Hi! Hang on." She glanced over her shoulder and then slipped down another flight of stairs. In a moment, she was outside in the muggy August heat. She leaned back against the brick. "It's...it's really great to hear from you. How did you find me?"

"Your name and newspaper were on your press

badge. I found your cell number on the newspaper website. You're a reporter, right?"

She glanced at the windowsill above. "I am."

At least until Monday.

There was a pause on the other end of the phone. "Is there any chance you could you meet me for coffee? I'm looking for advice about talking to the press…and you're the only reporter I know."

"Sure. Of course." She pressed her lips together and hoped she already knew the answer to the question she was about to ask. "About what kind of story?"

She heard Daniel take in a long breath and let it out slowly.

"It's about Brian Leslie's murder."

THREE

Heat shimmered off the highway like a mirage. The weather report had predicted dangerous thunderstorms all weekend. Olivia glanced at her cell phone. It had been about an hour and a half since she and Ricky had left Toronto and started north, and her cell phone signal was down to just one bar. A rundown motel and camping trailer park loomed ahead. A giant tattered clown sign told them to take the next exit for their fairground.

She shivered. "I think we turn here."

They pulled off the rural highway onto a smaller country road. When Daniel had told her that he'd be at his house in the country until some time next week, she'd decided it was better to offer to drive up there to meet him right away, instead of telling him she might be unemployed by the time he came back to the city.

When she'd told Ricky, he'd immediately offered to drive up with her, even though she suspected he might have blown off a weekend assignment from Vince to help her. An uneasy feeling was fluttering in her chest. She hadn't told Vince about the call from Daniel or that she was going to meet him. But Daniel had stressed he just wanted to meet for coffee to get her advice, nothing more. This wasn't an interview. This was just coffee. Still, no matter how hard she tried to convince herself that driving up to meet Daniel wasn't really the same as slipping off to the courts in the middle of the day without telling Vince, the unsettled feeling inside her wasn't convinced.

The thin rural road snaked past abandoned barns and ramshackle buildings, ragged from years of neglect. Broken windows peeked out from empty farmhouses. An empty strip mall loomed on her left, surrounded by a crude chained-metal barrier fence.

It was practically a ghost town.

"I can't tell if we're lost or not." Ricky glanced at his cell phone. "I've got no signal now."

They probably had another half hour before the sun began to set. Without streetlights there was no telling how dark this road would get. Then she saw a red-and-white awning ahead on her left next to a faded sign offering gas. A sigh of relief left her lungs.

"I think that's it." A bright green pickup truck sat on the edge of the gravel parking lot. There was fresh glass in the back window and bullet holes in the tailgate. "Actually, if you could pull just past the lot and park down the road a bit, that would be great."

Ricky did so. "Everything okay?"

"Absolutely. Daniel just seemed really hesitant about whatever he wants to talk to me about. He must have stressed three times that this was going to be nothing more than a casual chat over coffee, and that this needed to be private. So I don't want to spook him by showing up with a photographer, even if you're mostly just here as a friend."

"Got it." Ricky grinned. "Actually, would you be

okay if I drove back down the road a bit and tried to find a cell phone signal? I'd like to call my folks. They live about half an hour north of where we turned off the highway. If that megastorm hits early, we might be able to crash there tonight instead of driving back into the city."

Dark clouds had already started to gather at the horizon. If the storm really was as bad as forecasters feared, the road back to Toronto might even flood. Might make sense to drive north and wait until the roads reopened. But the worst of the rain wasn't supposed to hit until well after midnight. Surely they'd be back home long before then.

"Sure, just don't be gone too long."

"I won't. Just going to drive back to the creepy clown motel. Shouldn't take me more than thirty minutes. Forty tops."

"Sounds good." She got out of the car and walked toward the truck stop. Humid air tickled her skin. Bells clanged gently as she stepped through the doorway. Daniel was sitting at a table by the window. He looked up and gave her a slight wave. An unexpected shiver ran down her arms. She couldn't remember the last time she'd felt this nervous about meeting someone for coffee.

Get hold of yourself, Olivia. This isn't really "meeting a guy for coffee." It's hardly a date. He's a potential story source and witness to a murder.

She smiled professionally and started toward him, memorizing him down to every last detail. He had broad shoulders and strong arms. His plaid shirt was faded and the top two buttons were open. Dark eyes like mocha gazed straight into hers, with a look that was friendly yet also determined not to let her too deeply inside. He was unconventionally good-looking, with the air of a man who was used to keeping secrets.

Who are you, Daniel Ash? And how are you connected to Brian Leslie's murder?

"Olivia! Hi!" He stood. He was taller than she'd realized. At least six foot four. Maybe taller. His hand reached for hers. "It's wonderful to finally meet you, properly."

His smile was warm. Unexpectedly, she could feel a genuine smile tugging at the corner of her own lips, too. "It's honestly really nice to meet you, too."

They shook hands. His grip was surprisingly gentle. "How are you feeling?"

"I'm just fine. Thanks to you." She felt herself blush. "You saved my life."

"Don't worry about it. I'm just glad I was there."

Yes, but *why* had he been there in that parking garage?

They sat. For a moment, she didn't know what to say. How could she simply press him for information knowing that the last time she'd seen him, he'd cradled her into his arms and carried her to safety? Yet how could she feel this close to a man she knew practically nothing about? *Come on, Olivia. Think like a reporter.* "Well, I'm glad you knew what to do. The whole thing was like something out of a nightmare. Am I right in remembering you said you were a bodyguard?"

He nodded. "I used to be, yes."

"So you're a fighter, then?"

He laughed, a warm chuckle that seemed to roll off his shoulders. "I'm anything but. When you're a head taller than most people, with muscle to match, you learn it doesn't take a lot to hurt them, even without meaning to. The way I saw it, my job was to de-escalate violence and get my clients away from bad situations, not escalate trouble. So I'd use force, obviously, but only wisely and only when needed. Other bodyguards used to joke that I didn't actually need weapons, I just needed to stand there and look imposing. Used to call me the gentle giant."

"No weapons, huh?" Her gaze dropped to his muscular arms, now resting on the table. There was so much she wanted to know. "So you're not into guns?"

He frowned. "I don't have a license to carry a handgun or anything like that, if that's what you're asking. I do own a shotgun, though. But just for hunting birds."

He looked bothered by the question for some reason. She changed the topic back to the safer territory. "How long were you overseas?"

"Oh, years." He ran one hand through his hair. "When I was still in high school, I got a security job for a company here. By the time I was twenty-one the boss was taking me with him on business. I was always pretty tall and I used to have a full beard, too, so I guess I looked pretty scary. Then I got hired by a personal security company overseas. Mostly I'd escort foreign businesspeople around and keep them out of trouble."

"That's amazing." Fragments of him speeding through the smoke-filled garage flickered in the back of her mind. "Did you ever escort any journalists?"

"A few. Mostly in and out of war zones."

Wow. "Sounds dangerous."

"Sometimes." He shrugged. "It's only really dangerous if the person you're protecting doesn't follow directions. When someone's protecting you it's vital you're able to do what you're told without argument. The last thing you want is someone freaking out and running off madly. I mean, sometimes running is what keeps you alive. But sometimes running can get you killed, if you run in the wrong direction. A lot of the time, I had to subtly alert people of danger without causing them to panic, or even ask questions."

She leaned forward. "Can you give me an example?"

"Of how I'd warn someone of danger?" he asked. "Okay, your initials are OB, right? Say we were together and I spotted something. I might tap out your initials in Morse code on a surface, or even on your arm."

His fingers hovered over her wrist for a moment, like he was about to tap lightly on her skin. Then he pulled back and tapped the table beside it—one long beat, three short, three long. She watched his fingers as they moved.

"I can't imagine why you'd ever give up that life to come back to Canada."

She looked up. Something flickered in the depths of his eyes. *Sadness maybe? Regret?*

Then he blinked again, the unguarded flash of emotion was gone and only the politeness of an acquaintance remained. "Carpentry has always been a passion of mine, too. So I was happy to be able to pick up a hammer again. Being back gave me a chance to rebuild an old house that a relative left me, not far from here."

None of which even began to answer her question. A waitress dropped two menus on the table then left without so much as a nod. Over half the items were crossed off. Another long pause spread out between them. Whatever Daniel had wanted to talk to her about, he wasn't in a hurry to bring it up and he'd sounded so hesitant on the phone she hated the idea of pushing him. As much as she suspected she'd probably quite enjoy just listening to his stories for hours, they were hardly here for small talk. Ricky's printout of the Faceless Crew website was folded inside her notepad. She slid it out onto the table but didn't unfold it.

There really was no easy way to ask this. "Were you working for Leslie Construction, then? Either as a carpenter or as some kind of security?"

He sat up straight. Not surprising, considering she'd basically just asked if Brian had stolen from him or if the man had been killed on his watch. Or both.

"No." He shook his head, as if the question surprised him. "No, not at all. I mean, I did a handful of shifts for Leslie, here and there, a few years back when I needed a bit of extra money. Mostly I'm an independent contractor."

Now they were both surprised. "Then, why were you in the garage during the trial?"

"I was hoping to have the chance to have a quick word with Brian in private."

Her eyebrows rose. "About what?"

"A personal matter." His mouth set in a grim line, as though she was stepping over the line of whatever he was willing to let her know. He leaned back and crossed his arms in front of his chest. "What do you know about the Leslie family?"

There was an edge to his voice. It was as if he was testing her in some way she couldn't put a finger on.

She flipped her small notepad open, even though she knew what her notes said without even having to glance. "I know that Leslie Construction was started by Brian Leslie's father sometime in the early seventies. When he died, the company passed down to Brian and his sister, Mona. Mona had a reputation of being quite the party girl and got arrested on a handful of drinking and drug-related charges. But the crew generally liked her. They weren't so fond of Brian, who took over full ownership of the company when Mona died about four years ago."

The look of Daniel's face was serious, focused and inscrutable.

She kept going. "Brian had a gambling problem and tried to both cheat on his taxes and steal from his employees. But he wasn't very good at it and got caught. The court changed its mind about prosecuting him before the trial even started. We saw him get murdered. Now Brian is dead, the company is in shambles and will be passed down to his teenage niece, Sarah." She leaned back. "Now here I am talking to you." *And you won't tell me why.*

Another pause, then Daniel let out a long breath. "Okay. So that's a bit more than I was expecting. But a good starting point. Anything else?"

"Just this." She unfolded the printout about the Faceless Crew website and pushed it toward him. His eyes scanned the page while her eyes searched his face. It paled. "A colleague found this online. I don't know if this has any connection to Brian's murder."

"I've never heard of them before. Which is worrying. Maybe even terrifying, considering they might be after—" His words cut off abruptly. He ran both hands over his face, and for a moment it sounded as if he was praying under his breath. Then, to her surprise, he leaned across the table and took her hands in his, as if they were gearing up for something. "Okay, you've got to promise me that everything I'm about to tell you is off-the-record. All of it. At least for now. I'm trusting that this won't suddenly all end up in your newspaper."

She looked down at his hands holding hers. "You have my word."

A light flashed outside, illuminating the window beside them in a blinding blur of yellow and white. She turned to look, but all she could see were the spots of light dancing before her eyes. "Is that lightning? Already?"

"No! Someone out there is taking pictures of us!" Daniel leaped to his feet. Frustration flashed like fire through the depths of his eyes. "Please tell me you didn't bring a photographer with you."

Her heart sank. Oh, no. What was Ricky thinking? "Well, yes, sort of. But it's not what you think—"

Before she could even finish, he stormed past her and rushed outside.

Daniel scanned the parking lot just in time to see a shadow run off down the road. Moments later, he heard a car door slam. Then he saw headlights flicker on through the trees. Olivia's photographer colleague seemed to be just sitting in his car, probably waiting for her. Daniel stifled a growl. The sun had all but set now, leaving a wash of inky gray and black in the clouds above his head. The air was damp with the threat of impending rain that still seemed reluctant to fall. Tension rolled over his shoulders and back.

What had she been thinking bringing a photographer without telling him?

No, what had he been thinking in trusting a woman he barely knew when his stepdaughter's life was on the line? Keeping Sarah safe was his primary responsibility. Now more than ever.

It had been a very long time since he'd felt his mouth go that dry when he'd looked in a pair of sparkling eyes. Olivia was right when she'd called Mona Leslie a likable party girl. As an awkward, introverted eighteen-year-old mourning the recent death of his parents, he'd been instantly drawn to Mona's unpredictable energy and vitality. She'd been seventeen then, raising baby Sarah all on her own. They had provided him with an instant family—one that needed him. He'd married Mona when he was nineteen. But she'd never made good on her promise to give up drinking, drugs or fooling around. She'd left him less than two years later, announcing she wasn't cut out for monogamy. He'd taken a job on the other side of the world.

Still, when he'd gotten that long-distance call from a lawyer telling him that Mona was dead, that they'd still been legally married and he was still listed in her will as Sarah's legal guardian, he'd returned home. How could he let the child he'd once pledged to raise as his own end up in the care of social services? Mona might not have loved him for very long, but her decade-old will had specified that Daniel was the only person she trusted to be Sarah's guardian and to hold her inheritance until she turned eighteen. Even Mona had known not to trust Sarah's future to either her heavy-partying friends or her thieving brother, Brian. The bright-eyed baby who'd captured his heart long ago might now be an emotional, complicated teenager. But she was still his responsibility.

There was the clatter of the door opening and closing behind him.

"I'm sorry." Olivia was at his shoulder. Her voice was soft and filled with regret. "Ricky is a friend from work. He drove me up so I wouldn't have to come alone. Yes, he's a photographer. But I never expected he'd just start taking pictures."

He nodded to show he'd heard her, but still gave himself a few moments to calm back down before responding. After all, he'd been the one who'd decided to call her about the current crisis Sarah had found herself in. Ever since Brian's trial began, the teenager had received dozens of calls from nosy reporters, who just saw her as some kind of pretty novelty from a notorious family. Those calls had tripled since Brian's death. Daniel was exhausted from arguing with her on why throwing herself into the spotlight was probably one of the worst things she could do.

But when he'd told her about Olivia, Sarah had seemed open to meeting her, even though she'd been less than excited about the idea being interviewed by such a small newspaper. It had sounded as if it could be a workable compromise to get her story out without throwing her to the media wolves. He'd hoped meeting Olivia for coffee, explaining the situation with Sarah and getting her advice would be the first step in finding a sensible way forward. Instead, even just being around her made him feel strangely flustered.

The diner's light turned off. He glanced back. Someone had switched the door sign from Open to Closed. Moments later, the waitress and a second woman who he guessed was the cook walked out and drove off without so much as a wave in their direction.

He waited until they were gone before replying, "You should have told me he was here. I made it pretty clear that I wanted to talk to you off-the-record." Daniel turned and walked toward his truck.

"You did. And again, I'm sorry." Olivia followed and in a moment was walking by his side. "Ricky's young and he must have misunderstood me somehow. He dropped me off and told me he was planning to drive to find a cell phone signal to call his folks."

"And instead he parked down the road, sneaked back and snapped a picture, then ran off back to his car. These are hardly the actions of an honest person." He tried to keep his tone level, but irritation still seeped through his voice. This situation was ludicrous and exactly what he'd hoped to avoid. While he'd only shared a few brief moments with Olivia, it had still felt as though they'd had some kind of connection. That there was something deeper beneath the surface—maybe his faith, his worldview or his drive to do the right thing—that she'd shared, too.

Obviously he was wrong.

"Well, that's my fault, too, I guess," she said. "I'd asked him to pull past the diner when he dropped me off. So he must have done the same when he came to pick me up."

He stopped short. "So I wouldn't see him, right?"

"Yes, and I'm sorry." She crossed her arms in front of her chest. "I don't know how many times I can say it. I made the wrong call. I get now that this is apparently a big deal for you."

No, she didn't get it. He'd been ready to trust her with something more important than she could have known. And she'd blown it.

But she'd admitted she was wrong and she'd apologized. That was far more than Mona had ever done. True. But she was also a stranger and a journalist. And the way he kept comparing her to his deceased former wife was reason enough to get out of here quick.

"I'm sorry, too. This was obviously a mistake." He pulled his keys from his pocket and headed for his truck's driver's-side door. "I accept your apology. But this just doesn't feel right to me anymore. Please consider everything we have talked about off-the-record and don't contact me in future."

He watched her face, expecting her features to fall in disappointment. Instead, her shoulders straightened and a firm, clear determination flashed in their depths.

"Understood. Well, I'm very sorry to have wasted your time." She turned on her heel and started toward where the photographer's headlights shone through the trees.

"Hang on. Let me at least escort you to your colleague's car."

"No, I'm fine on my own, thanks." She didn't even turn. "Good night, Mr. Ash."

Olivia walked out of the parking lot without looking back. He climbed into his truck and tried not to watch her go. Part of him wanted to pray, but couldn't begin to find words for the jumble of thoughts racing through his mind. Another part of him wanted to run after her and apologize, not even knowing what he should be apologizing for. Instead, he waited a few minutes to give her the chance to reach her coworker's car. He heard a car door slam. A dark car sped past the lot. Seemed Olivia and her photographer friend were in a hurry to leave.

Daniel sighed, then eased his truck out onto the road and started driving. Despite the threat of rain, he rolled his window down and leaned out into the warm, damp night, hoping the fresh air would clear his head. What was it about this woman that unsettled him so much? He barely knew her, and yet sitting in the diner it had felt as if she'd been determined to reach around his defenses and rattle every single one of the locked doors inside him.

The headlights ahead of him lurched suddenly, weaving across the road and back as though the driver had suddenly lost control of the wheel. The dark car swerved toward the fenced-in remains of what was once a strip mall, then back onto the road again.

Olivia flew backward out of the passenger door.

FOUR

Daniel jammed on his brakes. The sound of his own thudding heartbeat filled his ears.

The world slowed.

Olivia's body tumbled along the road like a rag doll.

The dark car spun around so quickly it nearly swerved off the road.

She forced herself to her feet and started running away.

Her hands were bound behind her.

She'd been kidnapped.

A figure in fatigues leaped out of the car and ran after her. A mask covered his face. There was a gun in his hand.

Daniel pressed his foot to the gas.

Lord, help me save her. I can't fail her now.

He aimed the truck for the gap between Olivia and her kidnapper, planning to swerve between them and yank her in via the driver's-side door, using the truck to shield her from the gunfire. But Olivia turned, darted through a gap in the barrier fence surrounding the strip mall and ran toward the abandoned buildings. *No!* Daniel gritted his teeth. Didn't she realize those were *his* headlights shining on the road in front of her? Didn't she see that he was there for her?

If only he hadn't asked Olivia to meet him somewhere this isolated.

The masked thug leaped through the opening in the fence after her. Okay, new plan. Daniel swerved hard and came to a stop inches before the metal barrier. The masked man turned back and looked at him. Daniel's eyes searched his form. Black fatigues. No insignia. Same as what he'd seen in the parking garage. Could've come from any military surplus store.

Semiautomatic handgun. Popular and illegal.

So probably a low-level street thug.

His voice was gravelly and definitely fake. "Keep driving, old man. This doesn't concern you."

The masked thug leveled the barrel of the gun right between Daniel's eyes. Right, as though he was that easy to intimidate. He had faced down bigger guns and nastier threats back when this kid was probably still in grade school. Not that Daniel was about to be reckless and get himself shot while Olivia was still in danger. Daniel held the man's gaze just long enough to watch Olivia disappear between two buildings behind him. Showdown over. He shifted the truck into four-wheel drive and pulled away. The gunman laughed, turned and ran after Olivia.

Thunder rumbled in the darkened air. The skies opened. Rain fell with a vengeance.

Daniel gunned the engine. He raced past the fenced-in lot, then turned hard into the empty field. The truck bounced and jolted over the grass and scrub, kicking up mud in his wake.

A gunshot sounded from the lot to his left. Thankfully, whoever had condemned this strip mall had only thought to put barricades at the front of it. He turned hard and raced back toward the lot, hit a drainage ditch and launched the truck up onto a patch of pavement behind the buildings. Then he cut the engine and waited. Hopefully the gunman was too focused on his hunt to notice Daniel's little stunt drive.

Okay, Lord, now how do I—

But before the prayer could leave his lips, he saw Olivia shoot down an alleyway straight toward him.

She ran, barely able to see where she was going. Rain fell fast and wild, obscuring her view. The wind tossed her soaked hair into her face. Bonds dug into her wrists. Pain shot up her arms.

Her body smacked hard against the hood of a truck.

She gasped. The vehicle was nothing more than a gray shape in the darkness and had seemed to come out of nowhere. The driver's face was hidden in the darkness and distorted by water pounding off the windshield. She spun on her heel.

"Olivia!" a deep voice yelled. "This way."

She stumbled. A strong arm grabbed her around the waist and nearly hoisted her feet off the ground. She opened her mouth to scream. A hand clasped over her mouth. A breath brushed against her ear. "It's me, Daniel. It's okay. Just get in the truck." He half steered, half pulled her toward the passenger door.

Daniel? The complicated and moody man who'd told her never to contact him again? Could she trust him? Then again, she'd foolishly thought the blinding headlights she'd been heading toward had belonged to Ricky's car, until a masked man had stepped out of the shadows and pressed a gun into her face. If he was still after her, entrusting her safety to Daniel was the only choice she had left.

She tossed her head and his hand slipped from her lips. "Untie me. Now. And take me back to the diner."

"I can't. Sorry." Authority rang through each syllable as though she was just supposed to take his word for it. "Just get in."

"What do you mean you can't?"

With one hand, he reached around her and opened the passenger door.

"Just get in. I'll explain when we're out of here." Then before she could answer, he grabbed her waist with both hands and hoisted her into the truck. She landed on the seat. He reached past and buckled her in before she could even process what was happening. Then he slammed the door, leaving her sitting almost sideways, belted into his truck, her hands still tied behind her back. Daniel ran around and hopped into the driver's side. His wet shirt was plastered to his skin. Water streamed down his face.

Her voice caught in her throat. "I said, untie my hands and take me back to the diner."

"I said, I can't." He started the truck.

The thug who'd abducted her burst out of a gap in the buildings ahead of them.

A gunshot split the air, the sound fading into the echo of another thunderclap.

Daniel gunned the engine and threw the truck into Reverse.

They flew backward into a field.

"Diner's closed," Daniel said. "I'm taking you somewhere safer."

"But Ricky will come back to the diner looking for me!"

Another shot sounded in the distance.

"You sure your pal's coming back for you? Someone took our picture. And who else had any idea where you were? For all you know, he had something to do with what just happened to you." Tires spun in the mud. Windshield wipers slashed back and forth through the downpour. They were hurtling across a field into dark and empty nothingness. Did he even know where he was going?

"You can't possibly suspect Ricky had anything to do with that!"

Daniel stared straight ahead. "It's my job to suspect everyone."

"*Was*. Was your job. You're not my bodyguard. I'm not some helpless debutante who needs you to chuck me into your truck and make all the decisions for me."

One eyebrow rose. But he didn't even answer. She pressed her lips together and stared at the water pouring down the window beside her. Okay, that probably sounded pretty ungrateful considering he'd just saved her life. Again. But since he'd been the one who'd suggested they have some secret meeting in the middle of nowhere, it was probably his fault that her life had been in danger, too.

"I'm sorry, but I don't have anything I can cut your ties with here." Daniel drove up a steep incline. They bounced through a drainage ditch and hit another field. "I do have a utility knife with me. But I'd have to stop the truck to get at it. Since those are heavy-duty plastic zip tie cuffs, it would take me a couple of minutes to hack my way through them. Under the circumstances, getting away from whoever just tried to kidnap you is my top priority.

"Also, it would take me half an hour to drive to the closest police station, and I made the call not to head back to the main road because if that thug has backup that's probably where it would be waiting for us. But my place is less than three minutes from here and it's not on the kind of road a stranger could just stumble on easily. Once we're there, I can snip off those cuffs and we can call the police. Now, did that answer all your questions?"

Pretty much. "Enough for right now."

"Great." A wry grin crossed his lips. "And for the record, considering you just managed to escape from a moving vehicle while some thug had a gun pointed at you, *helpless* and *debutante* probably aren't quite the words I'd use."

Hang on, was that a compliment?

He risked a sideways glance. "I must admit, I'm kind of curious how you pulled that off."

Looked like it was. They came out on a thin, unlit road. The rain slowed to a steady patter.

"Well, I didn't realize it wasn't Ricky at first," she said. "By the time I got close enough to see it wasn't his car, someone had already stepped out of the trees, covered my mouth and stuck a gun in my face. He ordered me into the car. Said if I didn't go willingly he'd stick me in the trunk. I played along, but the first second the gun wasn't pointed directly at me, I opened the door, swiveled on the seat and kicked him in the jaw."

"Impressive." The grin on his mouth spread all the way up to his eyes.

They pulled onto a dirt road and the truck slowed to

a crawl. Trees pressed up against the window. Lightning flashed across the sky. She looked up.

A stone farmhouse loomed in front of them. Derelict and deserted looking, the building was three stories tall, with a wide, sagging front porch. If this whole area was mostly a ghost town, then this manor was definitely the broken jewel of the battered crown. He drove past the house and farther up the driveway to a rather big and surprisingly modern-looking barn garage. At the press of a button clipped to his visor, the garage door rolled up. "Welcome to my home."

They pulled out of the rain. The door rolled shut behind them.

"The house itself isn't much to look at yet." He turned off the truck and climbed out. "I'm restoring it from the ground up. Just the kitchen, one bedroom and the study are livable so far. The living room's nothing but a foundation pit and the whole second and third floors are structurally unsound. I still spend most of my time at my apartment in the city."

She scanned the garage. Rows of both antique and modern tools were arranged over a reclaimed wood workbench. Piles of lumber lay neatly stacked against the wall. He walked around the truck and opened her door. The gentle smell of sawdust filled the air. "I built the garage before I started gutting the house. There's a loft over the workbench, which doubles as both storage and sleeping space."

She glanced up. A thick wave of wet red hair tumbled over her face.

"May I?" he asked. She nodded. He brushed the hair gently behind her ear. Then he unbuckled her seat belt.

"I'm really very sorry to leave you sitting in those cuffs so long. Come on. Let's get them off you."

She started to step out of the truck. Her left foot snagged on some kind of strap underneath the passenger seat. She tumbled forward. Her body fell against his chest. His arms wrapped tight around her.

"It's okay, I've got you." He set her on the ground.

A flush rose to her cheeks. "My foot's just caught on something."

She looked down and sucked in a breath. It was the *Torchlight News* camera.

FIVE

"My camera! I was taking pictures with it in the parking garage just before Brian was shot!" If there were photos of the Faceless Crew on there, Vince would be sure to run them on the front page of the paper. Then, the police would have to take Vince seriously when he pressured them to answer their questions, and her place in the *Torchlight* family would be secure.

"Sorry, I didn't realize it was there. I thought I'd handed over all of your stuff at the hospital." Daniel picked it up. The lens was cracked and the view screen was smashed. "Pretty badly damaged, but hopefully the police will still be able to get something from it."

"I'll give it to the tech wizards at the newspaper first thing on Monday. Or actually, maybe Ricky can work on it tomorrow. I'll ask him as soon I figure out where he's gone. Once we get downloaded whatever's on it, Vince will make sure it gets handed over to the right contact person within the police. He'll know the best channel."

Daniel set the camera down on the front seat of the truck and led her across the floor to the workbench.

"Except that now is no time to be thinking like a reporter. You've potentially got evidence of a murder.
What we need to do is we hand it over to an officer,
any officer. Right away. We can't afford to wait around
for your newspaper to do their thing."

She bristled. He might be a good foot and a half
taller than she was, but that was no reason to talk to
her like a child. "Yes. But you don't just hand over evidence to the police without making a copy of it. How
would that be responsible? You also don't just hand
something this important for a news story to any random cop, because they have no reason to ever give it
back to you and you're all but guaranteed never to see
it again. Not that I've got anything against the cops.
My sister, Chloe, is a detective. But there's a way that
journalists handle sensitive, potentially explosive information. They make a backup copy of everything.
They get their editor to send it up the correct channels."

Sure, she was in his garage, in the middle of
nowhere—not to mention her arms were practically
screaming in pain from the zip ties around her wrists—
but she was still a reporter. He was going to take her
seriously.

"Well, I'm sorry, but I don't have a computer here, I
don't have an internet connection and it's almost eight
o'clock on a Friday night. You're just going to have to
explain to your editor that I insisted we give the camera to police and there was no way to back up any of
the pictures." They reached the workbench. "Now turn
around and I'll cut the cuffs off you."

"Hang on." She practically dug her heels in. "You've
saved journalists' lives before when you were a bodyguard. You told me so back in the diner. So you've

probably been in an actual war zone and known with certainty that reporter you were escorting had pictures or video with them of a bombing or a terrorist attack. Maybe you've even been present for an interview with insurgents or with a tribal warlord. Right?" It wasn't a question. She could see the answer in his eyes. "Did you ever not trust their newspaper to handle that information professionally? Or say that you were just going to take their camera from them and hand it over to police?"

He frowned. "Obviously not. But this is different."

"Why? Why is this different?"

"Look, can't we just get your handcuffs off? You've got to be in pain."

"Fine." She was. She'd been practically gritting her teeth not to let it show. "But that doesn't mean I'm agreeing with you."

Thunder rumbled around them. Rain pounded the roof above.

"I get that." Dark eyes met hers. "Now, if you'll just turn around for me, I'm going to grab a knife and free your hands. Stay as still as you can, okay?"

He stepped behind her. She heard him pick something up off the table, then felt one strong hand grab both of hers and hold her firmly still. There was the quick flick of something brushing against her skin.

Her hands fell free. The relief that flooded through her body was so intense it almost knocked her breathless. "Thank you."

"No problem. Thank you for trusting me." Daniel gently turned her toward him. "Can you feel your fingers? How's your range of motion?"

She let him take her hands in his. Carefully, he

brushed his fingers along the insides of her wrists. Then he linked his fingers through hers and gently moved each wrist around in a circle before letting them drop. Pins and needles shot painfully up her fingers. But the sensation of blood rushing into her hands felt so good it more than made up for it. "I'm sore. But it's not that bad."

"I'm glad." His hands brushed her shoulders, as if he was debating whether or not to hug her. Then his gaze ran over her shoulder and out toward the house. "First things first, we call 9-1-1. The dispatcher will take down our details and get someone to call us back about giving a statement. Either they'll come here or we'll go to whichever station they tell us. Or maybe, because it's late, they'll take our statements over the phone. You tell the cops whatever you want. But when I'm giving my statement, I'm telling them about your camera. Fair?"

She nodded. "Fair enough."

He stepped back and picked a cordless phone up off the workbench. "We'll try this first. The battery is pretty low and there's a landline in the house if we need it. But I'd rather we call from out here."

"Why?"

Why stand out in the garage when he had a house right there, even if only a handful of the rooms were finished? Presumably, the kitchen had chairs they could be sitting on. If not a coffeemaker. But he'd already dialed 9-1-1 and within moments was talking to the emergency dispatcher, who passed him through to a police call taker. Daniel relayed the basic details of what had happened, along with his phone number and address. Then he handed her the phone and Olivia did likewise.

"Someone will call you back shortly to take further details." The call taker's voice was female, elderly and somehow managed to hit that perfect spot between professional and comforting. "They might schedule an interview with you for tomorrow instead of dispatching an officer to your location tonight, unless someone is in imminent danger. Are you somewhere safe right now? Do you feel certain that the threat has passed?"

Daniel walked over to the window and looked out at the rain.

Olivia studied the strong lines of his form. "Yes."

"Do you feel safe?"

She closed her eyes. Even with Daniel's back to her it was as if she could feel his presence in the room. "Absolutely."

The phone beeped to warn her that the battery was dying. She quickly ended the call. "They'll get someone to call us back. But I gave them my cell phone number, too. So if you'd be so kind as to give me a ride back to civilization, they can still reach us that way. I don't know where the closest bus terminal is. But there was some hotel on the highway where we turned off. The clown-themed one with a campsite and some kind of little fairgrounds? I could spend the night there and find my way back to Toronto in the morning."

"That place is a rat trap. Trust me, you want to stay away from that place."

"Okay. Then, what do you suggest?"

"Give me a minute. I'm thinking." His shirt was still so wet from the downpour it practically clung to him. While she had to admit soaking wet wasn't exactly a bad look on him, this was hardly a "fall into some strong man's arms" kind of moment.

She straightened her top, walked over to the truck and picked up the remains of the camera. It was the type of model where all the pictures were saved digitally on a memory card. But the card was wedged in and didn't want to come out. She pinched hard with her fingers and yanked it loose. It looked bent. She slid it into the pocket of her jeans. Hopefully, once she found Ricky, it'd still be possible to get the pictures off it.

"Well, I can't read your mind," she said. "So how about you start by telling me what you're thinking? I still don't know why you asked me to come out here and meet you, or why you were waiting for Brian Leslie in that parking garage."

Daniel ran both hands through his hair and for a second it looked as though he couldn't decide whether she frustrated or amused him. "I've got to go into the house to check up on something. Then we'll discuss where to go from there. It might be best if I just drive you all the way back to Toronto tonight." He started toward the garage door. "I'm sorry if this sounds rude. But the thing I've got to sort out is kind of personal and I'd feel more comfortable if you stayed out here. I'll be back in a second."

"Seriously?" She didn't even try to keep the indignation from her voice. "Look, I've been pretty understanding about respecting both your privacy and your boundaries. But don't you think asking me to hang out alone in your garage, in the dark, like some kind of stray when there's a house with at least a few usable rooms right there is pushing it just a little too far?"

The garage door rattled. There was a banging sound, as if someone was throwing his or her weight against the metal. The door rolled up slowly.

In an instant, Daniel had stepped in front of her, shielding her body with his.

Her body tensed, waiting to either fight or run. Her eyes stayed locked on the rolling garage door. A pair of sturdy brown boots. Skinny legs in tight blue jeans. Long flowing blond hair slipping through the hood of a raincoat. Beautiful full lips twisted in a scowl. Olivia gasped. Daniel sighed.

"Olivia, meet Sarah Leslie, Brian Leslie's niece." Daniel took a deep breath. "My ward and former stepdaughter."

"I was married to her mother, Mona, for about two years a very long time ago," Daniel said. Although considering she'd just left him and never sought a divorce, they were still technically married when she died. "I'm now Sarah's guardian."

Shock didn't even begin to describe the look that crossed Olivia's face. He regretted not telling her sooner. But Sarah could be temperamental, and while she'd seemed to really like the idea of meeting Olivia and being interviewed by her, he hadn't wanted to just waltz into the house with the reporter without first talking to Sarah and filling her in. She'd already been frustrated enough when he'd insisted they get out of the city for a few days.

"Legal guardian." Sarah's lips turned up in an expression that was halfway between a smile and a smirk. "See, the law's kind of fun when it comes to being orphaned. You can move out and live on your own at sixteen. But I can't touch a cent of my inheritance until I turn eighteen."

"So November," Olivia said.

He wasn't even sure Olivia realized she'd said that out loud.

"Yeah…" Sarah's eyes scanned Olivia's face. Then her gaze cut to Daniel. "So what is this? You pulled up ages ago, but instead of coming into the house you hide out here?"

She said it as though he'd done something wrong. As though she was the parent and he was a teenager who'd sneaked a date into the garage.

"Sorry." He extended one hand toward each of them. "Sarah, this is Olivia. She's the reporter we talked about. I know I'd told you we'd talk about it first before I saw about introducing her. But when I went to tell her about the situation, someone tried to attack her after she left the diner. So I brought her here to call the police."

Sarah's shoulders rose and fell. She might be three months away from turning eighteen, but somehow the giant hood and baggy coat engulfing her body made her look several years younger. Before he could say anything more, she turned and started back toward the house.

A long pause spread out in the garage. Olivia's face was still pale in the dim light. Her eyes stared out into the darkness beyond. The rain had tapered off completely. Either the heavy storm was no longer coming or the weather had decided to give them a break before it hit in full force.

"I never thought to check Mona's marriage records," Olivia said, more as if she was talking to herself than him. "I did try to find out who Sarah's legal guardian was. But that information was confidential. I just assumed it was Brian."

"I met Mona when I was eighteen and she was seventeen. Sarah was just a tiny baby then and Mona was struggling to cope. I felt needed. We got married when I was nineteen. She quickly decided she wasn't cut out for married life and left me for good when I was twenty-one. It all happened rather fast."

He ran his hand over the back of his neck. His heart ached faintly at the memory of a very old wound. Everything to do with Mona had been fast. It was a mistake he'd never make again.

"Four years ago, I got a call from her lawyer saying she'd died. I was in Egypt at the time and still don't know how he tracked me down. But Mona and I had never legally divorced. I believed I'd made a commitment to her forever so it never occurred to me to ask for a divorce, and for whatever reason, she'd never filed. Her will still named me as the person she hoped would take custody of Sarah. It also gave me guardianship of Sarah's inheritance, which was and is quite considerable. When I married Mona, I promised I'd do whatever I could to help her take care of Sarah. Mona never trusted Brian, and her closest friends on the construction crew had the kind of criminal backgrounds that made social services think twice. She didn't really have anyone else. So I came back."

It had been tense. Sarah had been barely more than a toddler when he'd left. Now, as a highly independent teenager who'd grown up surrounded by drinking and partying and had just lost her mother, Sarah had pretty much accepted his guardianship as a kind of necessary headache that kept her from falling into the foster system. He just hoped he'd done right by her.

"As you can imagine, Sarah's been getting calls nonstop from media outlets who want to interview her ever since Brian was arrested. They've tripled now that he's died. Being a typical media-generation kid, she's really eager to do some interviews. But she's so naive. She's angry at how her name is being trashed in the mainstream press and thinks no harm can possibly come going on a media interview blitz to set the record straight. She worked part-time in the office at Leslie Construction, so she thinks all the people Brian stole money from are really her friends. She knows they're upset, but she thinks they only hate her now because of some big misunderstanding and will forgive her once she explains none of Brian's actions were her fault. I'm not sure she gets that the kind of anger they're feeling won't blow over quickly. She's even talking of running the company herself."

He nearly rolled his eyes as he said it. What was she thinking? While his legal guardianship might end when she legally became an adult, he'd hardly be able to abandon her then, especially if she was trying to run that wreck of a company with no business education and precious little experience to call on. "So she thinks that all she has to do is call up some reporters, tell them she's a really a good person and then everyone will see her side and get off her back."

"Well, right now nobody knows what to make of her," Olivia said slowly. "A good interview in the press could do a lot to restore her reputation. Or it could backfire really badly. It all depends on how the reporter and media outlet spins it."

"Which is why I called you. I tried hiring a public-relations firm, but she hated that. Said it felt as if they were trying to control her. And once she turns eighteen I can't prevent her from talking to the press any way she pleases." Keeping her away from the drinking and partying lifestyle that had ruined her mother's life was exhausting enough, not to mention stopping her from sneaking out to meet up with whoever she was trying to date behind his back. "But she was open to talking to you. As a compromise. I agreed that if she liked the idea of being interviewed by you, I'd probably be okay with that. But now, judging by her reaction, I don't know what to think anymore. I'm beginning to think this was a terrible idea."

"I understand. But you told me you didn't work for Leslie Construction besides taking a couple of shifts here and there."

"And I was telling the truth. When I first came back to Canada I did a few one-off construction jobs to pay the bills. Between that and all the time I spent trying to track down Brian at his office and various worksites, I also know a lot of his regular guys and they know me. But I had nothing to do with how Brian ran the place. My only role as Sarah's guardian was to make sure he didn't touch her share of the inheritance. Recently, Brian wouldn't even take my calls, which was why I was waiting in the parking garage to talk to him about doing the right thing, for Sarah's sake." A sigh rolled from his lungs. He felt as if he'd handled this whole thing so badly. But he couldn't think of anything he could have done different. "I'm sorry I didn't tell you before."

"Really, it's okay. I understand." Her tone was sad, almost bordering on resignation, and something about it rattled him, like a tiny thorn that pricked inside his chest. Then her shoulder brushed against his arm and he looked down at her face. There was a warmth in her gaze. A brightness that drew a person closer, like a campfire in the cold. A damp night breeze brushed through the open garage door, sending her hair dancing around her cheeks. Now the pain in his rib cage was so sharp he could barely breathe without feeling it pressing against in his heart.

He didn't know why.

They walked down the long, sloping driveway in silence until they reached the house. The kitchen was huge, with warm pine cabinets he'd crafted himself and a beautiful wood floor. It was the first room of the house he'd finished, as eating cold food scooped out of tin cans had quickly lost its appeal. Sarah was standing by the counter pouring herself a cup of coffee. Olivia walked over to the reclaimed wood table. The two women eyed each other.

"The other phone is in the study, just through that door there." He pointed toward the living room door. "The study's finished, but you'll have to cross through the living room to get to it, and I'm afraid that room doesn't have a floor yet. You'll have to walk across some planks I set up over the foundation's pillars. It's only like a six-foot drop on each side. I didn't dig a basement, just a crawl space."

"Thank you."

"Between working to pay the bills and Sarah finishing school in Toronto, restoring the house has gone really slowly. Especially since I'm doing it all myself and pretty much just on the weekends. That door right behind you leads to the other room that's finished. Sarah's using it as a bedroom right now while I take the study. The big door beside the window is the staircase heading upstairs. It's really pretty if you like ornate wood. But trust me, you don't want to try climbing those stairs."

He didn't quite know where the impulse to give her the grand tour had suddenly come from. But Olivia just nodded.

Then she turned back to Sarah. A professional smile spread across her gentle lips. She stretched out her hand. "I'm really sorry, we weren't properly introduced. As Daniel mentioned, my name is Olivia Brant. I'm a writer for *Torchlight News*. Daniel and I met at the diner to discuss your situation. But someone tried to abduct me, and your stepfather was kind enough to come to my rescue."

"Former stepfather." The teenager ignored Olivia's outstretched hand. "I hope you thanked him for bringing you out to the absolute middle of nowhere, where there's no cell service or internet access. I, for one, know I feel so much safer being somewhere I can't go online or chat with my friends." Blue eyes, so much like her mother's, cut toward Daniel. "I've changed my mind and I'm not okay with this anymore. I flipped through those copies of the paper you gave me and decided the *Torchlight* is not my thing. It's a ragtag small-time paper and Olivia doesn't even have any good bylines." She glanced vaguely in Olivia's direction. "No offense."

"None taken." Olivia pulled her hand back and crossed her arms. "I assure you, though, that you can trust *Torchlight News* with your story. While my paper might be small, it's honest, and I know a fair bit about your family and the case against your uncle."

What must she think of him now? Knowing he once

married Mona Leslie? Knowing he hadn't petitioned for a divorce after she'd left? That he'd then kept his youthful promise to his unfaithful former wife to protect her daughter all these years? The baggage of his past felt so heavy at times, and even with Sarah turning eighteen, there was no real end in sight. She still needed him, whether she wanted his help or not. He was bound to the choices he'd once made. And now he was the last kind of man who a woman would ever choose to build a life with, no matter how much his battered heart seemed to want to tug him toward Olivia.

"I really need to try to call my colleague to let him know I'm okay." Olivia's voice cut cleanly through his thoughts. "Also, the police should be calling back soon."

"There's a lamp just inside the office door. There are spotlights on the basement floor, too. They run on a basic extension cord." He opened the door to what would someday be a large beautiful living room but was now just a nicely dug pit surrounded by cool stone walls. A pathway of planks lay balanced across the foundation posts. She glanced into the gloom, then crossed the boards without once hesitating or looking down.

Sarah turned back to her coffee. "I don't like her. Her newspaper is small and boring, and I don't like how she looks at you."

Where was all this coming from? How exactly did she think Olivia looked at him? Daniel blew out a frustrated breath, and reminded himself that despite her brash exterior, here was a young woman who'd lost her mother barely four years ago and was now reeling from the death of her uncle. He glanced to the ceiling in silent prayer. *Lord, all I can do is advise and guide her. Help me find the right words to say.*

"I know you're old enough to make your own decisions," he said. "I just want you to be cautious and really think things through. Don't be too quick to dismiss Olivia. I think she's got a decent heart and isn't out to exploit you. Plus, she understands the stakes. She could've died in the same explosion and gun violence that killed your uncle, and someone just tried to abduct her at gunpoint—"

"Which should mean what to me, exactly?" Sarah folded her slender arms across her slight figure. "I mean, yeah, it's tragic and terrible, but there's no proof that any of it has to do with me, or even with Uncle Brian. She's a reporter. Someone could be after her for lots of different reasons. I'm just trying to live *my* life here, Daniel, and you're totally in controlling mode. I appreciate that you care and all, but just because you've cut me off from my friends and dragged me out here to your stupid construction project doesn't mean I'm actually in any kind of real danger. Whatever mess my idiotic uncle got himself into has nothing to do with me." She shook her head like a stubborn pony. "And just because you've now brought some pretty little journalist here doesn't mean I'm going to give her an interview."

The lamp was yellow, chipped and looked like the kind of relic one would find for fifty cents at a yard sale. But it was enough to cast a gentle glow in the room. A maze of rag rugs covered the cold stone floor. A paint-stained desk sat by the wall. She was almost surprised the clunky phone on top of it had push buttons instead of rotary dial. Olivia tried her answering machine first, half expecting to hear a panicked message from Ricky. There was only one message.

It was from her sister, Chloe. "Hey, little sis. I did some digging around into the Leslie Construction thing and I think you should find another story. Without going into details, that case looks big and messy, and there's more going on there than you can handle. We're talking about some pretty nasty people, and I don't want you getting hurt. So please—give this one up. Let it go. Let the people with the guns and the badges handle it. I'm sure your boss will understand and give you something easier. Okay? Call me back. Love you. Bye."

The phone went *click*. Olivia stared at it a moment, too stunned to even hang up. It was the first time she'd heard from her sister in weeks, and all she'd gotten was a lecture about how this story was too big for her to handle. She pressed her fingers against her eyes and blinked back hot tears.

Chloe had never taken her or her writing seriously. Six feet tall, athletic, top of her class in the police college, had always treated her artistic, five-foot-one little sister as some kind of cute little nuisance who couldn't take care of herself. While their dad's employment problems had kept them moving from town to town, Olivia hadn't just idolized her big sister—Chloe was the only friend she'd had. She'd been the one person who made her feel she wasn't alone. Until Chloe had left to join the Ontario Provincial Police.

Then I found the Torchlight News *"family." Which I'm about to lose, too, if I don't do something to prove to Vince that I should be allowed to stay. Besides, I've already faced my share of danger and survived—*

A sudden shiver ran down her spine as she remembered the feel of the thug's gun pressed up against her head. Yes, her sister could be overprotective, but surely Chloe wouldn't ask her to drop a story unless she was actually worried, would she? Except, it was too late now. She was right in the middle of this story whether Chloe believed she could handle it or not.

She needed to call Ricky. Fortunately, she could still access her address book on her phone even though she couldn't get a signal, so she was able to pull up his number and call him on the landline.

"Hey!" His voice echoed as though he was using his phone's hands-free setting. "Sorry, I know I'm running really late. I got a bit lost. Some cop pulled me over and then sent me on this ridiculous detour. But I think I'm on the right road now."

Ricky hadn't even made it back to the diner yet? She glanced up at a clock on the wall and blinked. It had only been an hour and a half since he'd dropped her off.

"Don't worry about it. I'm not at the diner anymore." She ran through the basics as quickly as she could— the masked man trying to force her into a car, heading back to Daniel's house, finding the photo memory card, meeting Sarah.

Ricky let out a low whistle. "Whoa."

"Yeah."

"So which of the three men was it? Brute, Rake or Shorty?"

There'd been so much going on she hadn't even thought to compare her attacker to the names and descriptions from the Faceless Crew website printout. "I don't know."

"Well, was he incredibly skinny, really short or built like a brick wall?"

"None of the above." She closed her eyes and tried to conjure up the gravelly-voiced man who'd pressed a gun to her face and threatened to shove her into the trunk of his car. "He was kind of on the large side, but nowhere near as big as the really huge masked guy I seem to remember shooting Brian. He did have a mask, but more generic, not one that matched the pictures of the Faceless Crew."

Did that mean the Faceless Crew weren't the killers—that she'd misremembered the men from the parking garage? She'd had a head injury and there had been a lot of smoke. Maybe it was only her imagination that the attackers resembled the Faceless Crew. Certainly the man from tonight hadn't matched any of the crew's profiles.

She sat down on the floor and leaned back against the battered couch. "I have no idea if Sarah's going to let me interview her. She says she's changed her mind about it, but I don't really know. She's young and kind of temperamental. Maybe I could use Daniel to get through to her."

But even as she heard the words leave her mouth, she felt guilty. Daniel had saved her life. How could she possibly think about using him to save her job? She glanced to the window above her head. The rain seemed to have stopped for now, but thick, humid air was pressing its way through the screen. *Get a grip, Olivia.* Daniel was nothing more to her than a potential source. She was nothing more to him than some random reporter who'd stumbled into his life, and was pretty close to tumbling right back out again. "Daniel is a really good guy, but he doesn't seem to care that as reporters we have a job to do, too. He's pushing me to turn the photo card over to the police right away, skipping Vince entirely, without even making a backup."

Not that she could entirely fault him now that she knew he was worried about protecting Sarah.

"Do you want me to go grab a laptop and see if we can download those pictures right away?" Ricky asked. "I'm sure I have a spare one at my folks' house."

"Yes! Absolutely." She sat up straight. That was perfect. "The diner's closed already and Daniel didn't seem that keen on that clown motel. But maybe he can suggest somewhere else he'd be willing to drop me off that we could meet up. Or we could meet back in Toronto really early tomorrow morning." It's not as if there could be a huge amount of difference between handing the pictures off to police at eleven-thirty at night or nine in the morning. She doubted cops would be working through the night on Brian's murder.

The phone's call waiting beeped. "I've got a call on the other line. It's probably the police. Go to your folks' house, and once I figure out where and when to meet up, I'll call you back."

"Sounds good. I just hope the storm holds off."

The phone beeped again. "I'm sure it'll be fine. Talk soon." She hung up and accepted the incoming call. "Hello?"

Breathing on the other line. Heavy. Slow.

"Hello? Anyone there?"

"Hey there, sunshine." The voice was male, raspy and deep. "Just want you to know that I know where you are and you're not going to get away from me so easily. I'm going to come hunt you down. And then I'm going to kill you."

SIX

Olivia slammed down the phone. Her whole body shook as though someone had just poured freezing water down her back.

It was him.

It was the voice of the man who'd pressed a gun to her face, tied her hands behind her back and threatened to toss her into his trunk.

Somehow he'd found her.

She leaped to her feet and pushed open the study door. Then she paused. Daniel and Sarah were arguing in the kitchen. Loudly. She forced a deep breath into her lungs and let it out slowly.

It didn't make sense. The call had come in on Daniel's home phone. How had the kidnapper known how to reach her?

The phone rang again. The loud noise reverberated off the walls around her.

Come on, Olivia. You're not Chloe's tagalong little sister anymore. You're a reporter. You're a strong, confident woman. If the man on the other end tries to intimidate you, just grab a pen and write down everything you can hear. Everything he says. Every bit of background noise...

The phone rang again. She snatched it up firmly. "Hello."

"Hello?" The voice was male. But also youthful, eager and earnest by the sound of it. "My name is Constable Henry. I'm with the Royal Canadian Mounted Police. Is this by any chance Olivia Brant?"

Oh. A cop. "Yes. Hi, I'm Olivia."

"Nice to meet you, Ms. Brant." Sounded as if the Mountie was smiling. "I'm sorry to hear of the difficulties you've experienced in the past couple of days and I want to assure you we're doing everything we can to see that those responsible are brought to justice. Now, would you have time to help me out by answering a few questions?"

She grabbed a small notepad and pen off the desk. "Absolutely. Just give me your phone number and I'll call you back."

Never could be too careful.

"Oh, no problem." He gave her his badge number, too. She wrote it down, hung up and called the number he'd provided. It rang through to a RCMP call taker who put her back through to Henry. Looked as if the cop was legit. Not that she figured anyone would fake being that chipper. Judging by the background noise, Constable Henry was on his cell phone.

"Okay, let's do this."

He started by taking her through the attempted kidnapping outside the diner, helping her remember every detail about the man who'd tried to take her by gunpoint. She told him about the terrifying phone call she'd just answered as well, and everything she knew about the so-called Faceless Crew. To his credit, he managed not to sound skeptical. Then he started asking her detailed questions about the day Brian died.

It was only then that she felt the hairs of suspicion rise on the back of her neck. The RCMP was Canada's *national* police force. A federal police officer had called her back, on a Friday night, to take her statement on an attempted kidnapping, barely half an hour after her initial 9-1-1 call. Just how often did that happen? She forced a professional smile into her voice. "Excuse me if this is an odd question, but why is the RCMP investigating this?"

"No problem." Henry's voice was so cheerful she couldn't help but imagine him wearing a bright red uniform. He probably even had freckles. "I'm part of an investigation that's looking into Mr. Leslie's murder and things surrounding it."

Which was the opposite of an answer. "So are you taking my statement about the kidnapping because I was a witness to Brian's murder, then? Does the fact the feds are investigating both his murder and my attempted kidnapping have anything to do with why the case against him was dropped? Tax evasion is a federal crime."

"I'm sorry, but I'm not at liberty to divulge information in an active investigation. I'm sure you understand."

"Absolutely." She did. But that didn't mean she wasn't still a reporter. "Can you at least tell me if you'd even heard of the Faceless Crew before I mentioned it? Or if you think this crime could be connected to any other car bombs or fires they've taken credit for?"

"I'm afraid I really can't say." The smile hadn't left his voice for a moment.

Again, fair enough. He was a cop after all, and she had no reason not to trust him. But it definitely felt as though something else was going on.

"It's getting pretty late," she said, "and I'm still hoping to return to Toronto tonight or at least find a good hotel. Would it be okay if we continued this at the newspaper offices on Monday? I'd really love to have my editor, Vince, sit in on this. I'm sure he'd be fascinated by it all."

Fascinated was one word for it. Vince had a healthy respect for cops as much as a marine biologist had a healthy respect for sharks. He admired them and could swim alongside them quite comfortably. But he was always quick to notice when the current shifted.

Headlights flashed through the window above her. There was the sound of tires on gravel and the hard but indistinct thumping of heavy music.

"Sure, sure," Henry said. "Thank you so much for your time, Ms. Brant. We'll be in touch soon."

A second set of lights brushed the window. She stood up and looked out. A cavalcade of vehicles and camper trailers were pulling into the driveway.

"Have a good night, Ms. Brant."

"You, too."

Constable Henry had already ended the call. A blare of horns filled the air. She stuffed the pen and pad of paper into her pocket and started down the planks toward the front porch.

Daniel flung the kitchen door open and ran outside. There had to be at least six vehicles now trying to find somewhere to park, including two motor homes and three trucks dragging camper trailers. Former members of Leslie Construction crews spilled out onto his lawn. Some carried coolers. Others had chairs. What was happening? He spun back toward the house. Sarah was standing in the doorway. "Tell me you didn't invite the crew up here for a party?"

Sarah craned her neck to look past him. "Are you kidding? They still hate me, remember?"

Some of them probably did, and not without reason. She was inheriting the company that had owed them a lot of money, and had wrecked some of their lives. He wouldn't be surprised if some of them had shown up here in an attempt to put pressure on her to make things right. Just how long were they planning on camping out? Until they were paid? Or until the police showed up and dragged them off?

He pointed Sarah toward the kitchen. "Go back inside and don't come out. Be prepared to call 9-1-1 if you have to. But I'm really hoping it won't come to that."

While he didn't want an attempted siege on his lawn, he wanted a bloody brawl even less. They'd be waiting forty minutes for the cops to show up, maybe even longer. That was plenty of time for things to get a whole lot worse. These people had driven a long way to get here. Knowing the cops had been called would only ratchet up the tension. For now, he was still hoping it would be possible to de-escalate things.

"Seriously? You want me to hide in the house?" Sarah practically shrieked.

Why must she fight him on everything? He turned back to the unexpected guests. Looked as if some of them were setting up to party through the night. Didn't look as if any of them had come specifically looking for a fight. "Yes. Head to my office, ask Olivia to stay with you and be prepared to call the police. Hopefully this is all just one big misunderstanding."

A massive one—considering how hard he'd worked for the past few years to protect Sarah from the Leslie crew's wild parties. Still, most of these guys were actually pretty decent. Even if two of them were now dragging a beer keg onto his lawn.

Lord, whatever's going on here, help me calm things down and not make things worse. Help me handle it the way You'd want me to.

"Hey! Where do you want the fireworks?" There were two young men at Daniel's shoulder—Connor and Jeremy. In their early twenties, they were either brothers or best friends—Daniel wasn't sure—and played in a local baseball league.

Daniel ran his hand over the back of his neck. "I'm sorry, I don't know what you guys have been told or by who, but there's no party here. I'm actually going to need to ask everyone to leave."

"Oh. Wow. Sorry, man." Jeremy frowned. "We brought tents. Heard it was going to go all night and figured we'd want to sleep off the booze somewhere dry before trying to drive back. Should've known Kendra got the weekend mixed up when the weather report said it was gonna rain."

"Kendra?" If Daniel remembered correctly, Kendra was the petite, pixie-haired nineteen-year-old Brian had hired as an intern shortly before he died. Definitely the type to get a bunch of hot-blooded young men driving out to the country for a night of hard partying and drinking.

As someone who loved the country, the fact that so many city dwellers only saw it as a place to drive to so they could party and "get wasted" on the weekend never ceased to drive him nuts.

Connor nodded. "Yeah. She texted. Said she'd heard there was something big going down for Brian. Sorry if we got our wires crossed."

Oh, there was something going down, all right. But it was probably a whole lot bigger than a teenage intern inviting people to an overnight drinking party.

"No worries," Daniel said. "But if you can pass the word along to the other guys, I'd appreciate it. There's a campsite and motel by the highway. I'm sure they'd be happy for you to party there."

"No problem." Connor nodded again.

Thank You, God. But something told him not everyone would be that easy to get rid of.

The music was still pounding and the heavy beat seemed to reverberate inside his head. As soon as he figured out which car it was coming from, he was switching it off. He strode down his crowded driveway, through the line of vehicles, nodding at everyone he recognized and politely asking them to leave. He'd start with them first and then move on to the ones who would really cause him trouble. Thankfully a couple of the trucks were already making their way off the property, even though it had taken cutting over his lawn to get around the vehicles parked behind them.

The music seemed to be coming from a small motor home covered in bumper stickers. Someone had set up huge speakers in the open doorway, with their cord running all the way to the cab radio. Daniel reached around the speakers and unplugged them.

"Get off my camper and tell me what you've done with my niece!" Rita Ryan was suddenly so up in his face that her work boots might as well have been planted on Daniel's toes.

Sarah's so-called auntie Rita wasn't actually a relation. The spiky-haired woman was Mona's drinking and drugs buddy since the old days, and the friend that his ex-wife had moved in with when she'd left him. While Daniel knew Mona was to blame for her own bad choices, it didn't help that Rita had been there, egging her along, every drunken step of the way.

He took a step back and crossed his arms. "Rita, you know you're not welcome here. Please leave. Don't make this any harder on Sarah than it already is."

"You don't get a say in what Sarah needs!" Rita's laugh was so harsh and angry that it sounded halfway between a yelp and a snarl. She jabbed a finger in his face. "You're not Sarah's real family. You're nothing but some piece of stupid that Mona hooked up with and used to help her raise her baby for a while. Sarah's good-for-nothing uncle just died. She's about to inherit way more money than a kid like her can handle. She needs her auntie Rita."

Daniel felt his teeth set on edge. There was a growl growing in the back of his throat. Sarah needed Rita's help how, exactly? To help spend her money? To help her run the company? To help get her hooked on drink and drugs?

"Someone like you is the last thing she needs." He glanced back to the house, hoping Sarah had listened for once and stayed inside. The kitchen door was closed. But the front door was wide-open. A handful of people were crowded on his sagging porch. The crowd shifted just enough for him to see what they were crowding around.

Olivia was standing right in the middle of them, somehow managing to look even tinier than usual compared to the mass of muscle and bulk surrounding her.

"Olivia!" he called out. "Get back in the house and find Sarah!"

But she didn't give any sign she'd heard him. He started across the lawn. Forget Rita. He had to get Olivia back inside the house. Not that he expected any of the men would lay a violent hand on her, but this wasn't her fight, and if Olivia got hurt he'd never forgive himself.

A heavy hand landed on his shoulder. Daniel turned back and came face-to-face with Rita's on-again, off-again boyfriend. A longtime member of Leslie's construction crew, Reginald Hawkins—better known as Hawk—was a big, bald man with arms full of badly drawn tattoos, including a giant bird of prey on his neck. Not to mention a rap sheet full of both assault and drug charges.

While Hawk wasn't the kind of man who'd go to the trouble of planning a tailgate party as an excuse to get his crew up here, he was definitely the type to grab any chance to get his own point across.

Hawk shoved his way into Daniel's chest. "Maybe Rita's not the only one who wants to see Sarah. Maybe some of us wanna see her, too. Maybe me and some of the guys here, want to congratulate the baby princess on inheritin' a company, and make sure she knows we're ready to get back to work." Hawk chuckled menacingly. A few of the larger louts behind him chuckled, too.

Okay, Lord, something tells me I'm really going to need Your help finding a way out of this.

He glanced back toward the porch, but couldn't see Olivia anymore.

"Yes, Sarah and I both know Brian died owing all of you a lot of money, and I promise you I'll do everything in my power to make sure you're paid back. But you're going to have to be patient. Things are going to be tied up legally for a while. We're going to need a lawyer to sit down and help us sort out who's owed what—"

"I'm done being patient!" Hawk's voice rose to a bellow. "That rat Brian died owing us weeks of pay! She's gotta answer for that!"

Daniel stood firm and held his ground. "You're right. Brian shortchanged your paychecks. But Sarah's just a kid, and it's going to take time to sort things out. You're just going to have to trust the process."

"Like we trusted Brian to do right by us? Like we trusted the courts to settle this?" Another laugh from Hawk, this one with teeth. "You think we're stupid? You think we don't know some lawyer can decide the company is too broke to pay us while pretty little Sarah still walks away inheritin' plenty of family assets? You think we don't know suing could take more money and years than we got? Some of us haven't worked in weeks. We got crew defaultin' on mortgage payments. We can't even get unemployment insurance, thanks to how Brian messed with the books." He leaned his bulk in so close, Daniel almost choked on the stench of his beer breath on his face. Hawk's lips curled up in an ugly sneer. "We're not going anywhere until we're convinced little Sarah understands just how important it is she makes things right."

SEVEN

Daniel's blood ran hot in his veins. *Lord, I don't want to have to fight this man. But I will, if it means keeping someone else from getting hurt.*

Another man stepped up behind Hawk. Younger, stronger, with wavy black hair and dangerous eyes. Trent something. Trent was much newer to the team, but seemingly cut from the same cloth as Hawk.

Hawk glanced at Trent and smirked. Two against one. Three, if Rita decided to jump in the fray.

Lord, I could really use some backup.

Hawk stepped forward. His knuckles cracked. Daniel raised his hands in a fighting stance and tensed his body to deflect a blow.

"Excuse me, Mr. Reginald Hawkins!" Olivia appeared behind him. Her voice was strong, professional and crisp enough to cut glass. "Isn't it true you actually asked Brian Leslie to keep your work off the books to help you avoid child support?"

Daniel's jaw nearly dropped. Something told him that nobody—not even his grandmother—ever dared to call Hawk "Reginald." Yet here Olivia was. A tiny, slender little spitfire of a woman, staring down a man three times her weight, who could probably level her in a single blow. Didn't she realize how dangerous the situation was? He bent his head toward her. "What do you think you're doing?"

"My job." Olivia's eyes glanced at Daniel, but she was making no attempt to lower her voice. "Did you know Hawk and some of the others were complicit in what Brian was up to?"

"No," he admitted. "Who told you that?"

"Some of the ones who weren't in on it. It's amazing what people will tell a sympathetic journalist when you know how to ask."

True. In all the years he'd worked in war zones he'd seen plenty of reporters risk their lives to simply ask questions. He'd accompanied them behind enemy lines and into the dens of warlords. A good reporter could get to the bottom of situations that seemed impenetrable. But he'd never felt his heart lurch quite the same way with any of them as it did at the sight of Olivia staring down Hawk armed only with a notepad and pen. Daniel's arm slid around her shoulders. His fingers tapped a Morse code warning on her bare arm, exactly as he'd tapped it out on the table when they were talking in the diner. Olivia froze. For a moment, he hoped she'd recognize his attempt to subtly warn her of danger and run back to the safety of the house. Instead, she just patted his hand.

Hawk looked Olivia over and muttered a swearword that made every muscle in Daniel's body tense with the urge to deck him in the jaw. "This your girlfriend, Danny boy?"

Olivia stretched her slender hand toward Hawk. He ignored the attempted handshake. "Olivia Brant, *Torch-*

light News. You and your friends were in the court-room just before Brian Leslie was killed in the parking garage, and you all looked angry enough to kill when the charges were dropped."

She nodded at Trent. "In fact, you were so upset, you had to be dragged off by police. It's Trent, right? No one I spoke to seems to even know your last name, as apparently all of the work you did for Brian was off the books. Wouldn't you all agree that since you gained the benefit of being paid under the table by Mr. Leslie, it's going to make it harder to determine just how much Leslie Construction actually owes you?"

A pen clicked in her hand, and somehow it managed to sound every bit as loud as the sound of the safety of a gun. Rita's face paled. Hawk swore under his breath. Both of them looked jittery enough to explode.

Only Trent stood calm. He eyed her for a long moment. Then he chuckled. "You are some gutsy piece of work, Ms. Brant. You know that? If you're not careful, one of these days you're gonna get yourself into some real trouble." Trent turned and sauntered toward a truck. Rita hesitated, then followed after him.

Olivia glanced at Hawk. "How about you? Any comment?" She glanced down at her notepad "I already have confirmation from two other people here that you actually pushed Brian to, and I quote, 'cheat those government pigs any way he could.' Certainly sounds as if you were supportive, if not complicit, in his actions, at least until you realized you were going to lose out."

"You're kidding me, right?" Hawk's eyes were so wide they were practically bloodshot. "So what if I worked a few jobs off the books or told Brian some little ways he could shave off taxes? Brian was our guy. He was supposed to be on our side and he cheated us!"

Olivia's pen moved across the page.

"Stop writing things down!" Hawk shouted so hard his voice nearly cracked. "Or I will punch you in your pretty little mouth."

"Except for the fact that with a rap sheet as thick and full as yours, you wouldn't want to risk the fallout for beating up a reporter." Her bright green eyes flashed with determination. That woman was fearless. "Don't even pretend for one second that everyone else up here would have your back. They just came here to party, not to watch you commit a felony."

Hawk turned around and only now seemed to notice his backup was gone.

Scattered raindrops hit Olivia's notepad, smudging the ink. Daniel pulled her closer into his side. He leaned his head toward hers. "Looks as if you've got some good stuff there. But now I'd feel a whole lot better if you'd go into the house and make sure Sarah's okay. This is a lousy place and time for you to go around trying to be a reporter."

She bristled and slipped out from under his arm. "I *am* a reporter."

"But you're not *just* a reporter, are you? You're also a…" His voice faded as he couldn't find the right word to finish the sentence.

"I'm a what, Daniel?"

You're a person I feel responsible for. You're someone I don't want to see get hurt. "You're a guest in my home and on my property. Please at least go check on Sarah and make sure she's safe."

She stepped back. A pair of taillights illuminated

her face for a second. Her mouth opened as if to argue. Then she closed it again. "Fine."

She started back toward the house.

"Hey, Hawk!" Trent hopped up on the tailgate of a truck. His hands cupped around his mouth. "A bunch of people are going to head back to that campsite and motel place. Come on, man. It's got clowns. This place is the pits!"

"Yeah sure. I'm in," Hawk called. "Just as soon as I teach this guy a lesson."

Hawk turned, raised his fist and charged toward Daniel.

EIGHT

Olivia froze just outside the kitchen door. Hawk charged toward Daniel, stumbling and bellowing like a drunken rhino. Daniel stood firm as though he was bracing to take the blow.

Dear Lord, please don't let Daniel get hurt—

Hawk swung. Daniel stepped sideways. He ducked under Hawk's fist, grabbed the bigger man's outstretched arm and twisted it, using the man's own momentum to throw him flat on his back. Hawk yelped, his arm now wrenched and trapped in Daniel's grasp.

Daniel stood over him. The night was eerily silent for a beat. Then Daniel's voice floated calm and clear through the muggy night air. "Now please get off my property."

Her heart skipped in her chest. His self-control was incredible. Impressive. Maybe even rather attractive. He glanced up her way for a moment, still standing there in the driveway with the thug who'd just tried to attack him pinned on the ground at his feet. Daniel's eyes met hers for barely a second with a look so raw and unguarded she could feel her already shaken heart speed even faster.

She pushed through the door to his kitchen. It was empty. She leaned her back against the door frame and pressed her palm into her chest. What was it with him? One moment he was capable of giving her a look that took her breath away. But just moments before, she had been absolutely infuriated with how deeply he seemed to need to control everything around him—including her. If she hadn't been out there "acting like a reporter" and asking questions, they might never have known that a handful of Brian's construction crew were complicit with his cheating scheme.

There was a heavy thud, followed by the sound of a muffled cry coming from behind the bedroom door.

She yanked it open. Sarah was pressed with her back up against a wooden dresser. A young man's hands were on her shoulders. For half a second, Olivia froze, thinking she'd interrupted a stolen romantic moment. But then Sarah's eyes, wide with a fear bordering on panic, met hers over his shoulder.

"Help me!" Sarah gasped, struggling to push him back. "Get him out of here!"

In three steps Olivia had crossed the tiny bedroom floor. "Back off and let her go."

"Drop dead," the young man replied with a snicker. "This doesn't concern you."

But Sarah's panicked eyes said differently. "Please, Jesse. Just leave."

"No."

Right. With one hand Olivia grabbed a fistful of Jesse's scarecrow-blond hair. With the other, she cuffed him hard in the side of the head, just enough to send his ears ringing. Then before he could react, she grabbed his ear like an errant child and yanked him backward. "Sarah says she wants you to go!"

Jesse stumbled backward and nearly fell into Olivia. A good, hard blow to the eardrum could knock even the toughest man's sense of balance into chaos.

"Let go of me, you stupid cow, or I'll beat you into the floor!" Jesse's hand raised to slap her. But before the blow could even land, Olivia kneed him in the gut, knocking him back just enough to lessen the sting of his fingertips striking her cheek.

"Jesse!" Sarah yelled. "Stop it! Please!"

But Jesse's hand clenched into a fist. He started to turn toward Sarah. Olivia kicked his back leg out from under him. He stumbled to his knees.

"Come on!" Olivia grabbed Sarah's arm and pulled her into the kitchen. "Let's get out of here!"

"Wait." She glanced back toward the bedroom. "Jesse could be hurt."

"I hope so!" Olivia's hand tightened on her arm. "Now come on!"

She started to throw her weight into the screen door. But it flew open from the outside. Olivia tripped over the ledge, dropped Sarah's arm and pitched headfirst into Daniel's chest. He caught her with both hands. The warm, woodsy smell of him filled her senses. His clothes were rumpled and his hair was damp with sweat like a man who'd just walked away from the right end of a fight. "What's going on?"

"It's not what it looks like, Daniel!" Sarah's tone was almost defiant.

Daniel let Olivia go. "It looks as though Olivia was trying to drag you outside."

Olivia retreated into the kitchen and glanced back to the bedroom door. Jesse was nowhere to be seen.

Daniel walked past her into the kitchen and over to Sarah. "Are you okay?"

Sarah shook her head. "Yes. No. I don't know. It all happened so fast. I didn't know what to do…"

Daniel dropped one arm over Sarah's shoulders and looked at Olivia. A hard, searching look crossed his face. "Do you want to explain what's going on?"

"No, let me." Jesse walked in from the bedroom and for the first time Olivia could get a decent look at the man. She pegged him as midtwenties. Messy hair that tried hard to be stylish, gray eyes and broad shoulders now slumped nonthreateningly like a dog trying to get away with something. *What an actor.* "Sir, I think I might owe your stepdaughter an apology."

"Might!" Olivia's voice rose. "You grabbed her!"

"It was a misunderstanding." Jesse shot her a dirty look. "Sarah and I were talking. I misread some signals and I think I accidentally frightened her."

Olivia's eyes flew up to the ceiling. "You threatened to beat me into the floor—"

"I didn't mean it. I was just running hot."

"You *hit* me!" Her voice rose.

So did his. "I barely touched you!"

Sarah was still standing there, watching the fight unfold without saying a word.

Jesse turned to Daniel. "Please, sir. You've got to believe me, this was just some big old misunderstanding. Everyone misread some signals and I apologize for my share of the blame. I certainly meant no harm. But that woman attacked me. I can't be blamed for losing it. She was totally out of control."

They were out of line... I can't be blamed for losing it... I was totally justified... They were out of control... Olivia stopped short as she heard her father's words echoing in her memory. How many times had she stood in some rented apartment kitchen, surrounded by packing boxes and listened as her dad explained he wasn't at fault for the fight that had cost him yet another job? No matter how many jobs he lost. No matter how many times the family had to move. She'd always believed him when he said he wasn't in the wrong, because what little girl wouldn't believe her daddy? Then she'd grown up thinking the world was full of volatile people, that everyone was at risk of suddenly losing their job for no reason and every good situation would be inevitably blown to pieces.

Except that just a few minutes ago she'd watched Daniel calmly hold his own and maintain self-control in the face of those thugs.

Olivia took a deep breath. "Daniel, I know how this looks. Jesse's right that I laid hands on him first. But he's lying about everything else that went down. He's the one who was way out of line. I was trying to protect Sarah."

For a moment it was as though the scene had frozen around Daniel in the same eerie, slow-motion way he used to assess a violent skirmish, looking for an exit. Sarah was pressed against his side. Jesse's hand was raised as if ready to strike Olivia's words right out of the air. And Olivia... She lit up his kitchen like a firecracker. Anger flushed her cheeks. A fierce, determined strength flashed in her eyes. He couldn't remember ever seeing someone more alive.

What happened here? Jesse Sinclair had always struck Daniel as the kind of quiet but arrogant guy who mostly kept to himself. The kind of man who pretended to be a gentleman instead of openly being a brute. Then again, too many others on the construction crew were the type to turn flirting into something that bordered on harassment. Just one of the many poisons that seemed to run in the Leslie company veins. But was Jesse really the kind of person who'd manhandle Sarah and Olivia? If so, why wasn't Sarah standing up for her? Could Olivia have blown this whole situation out of proportion?

But that particular train of thought stopped dead in its tracks as he let his gaze deepen on Olivia's face. It was pale, not from anger but from fright. He saw the slight tremor shaking her lips and the tears she was fighting to keep from falling from her eyes. His gut twisted into knots.

He may not have witnessed what had happened, but he could see the results as clear as day. Olivia was shaken, and deeply.

He kept his right arm lying over Sarah's shoulders and reached his left hand out for Olivia. "Are you okay? Did he hurt you?"

"Yeah." She nodded, but didn't take his hand. "I'm okay."

"Let me explain—" Jesse tried to slip between them.

Daniel's hand shot up before the young man could take another step. "Look, I don't know if you accidentally misread Sarah's signals or if you intentionally misread them because you didn't much like the message they were sending. But I don't actually care. Either way, you should be far more concerned with making things right than making a bunch of excuses, because there's *no* excuse for frightening either of them the way you did. Let alone actually laying a hand on Olivia!"

"Dude, it wasn't my fault." Jesse scowled. "That stupid cow was totally out of line."

So much for "sir."

"Get out of my house." Daniel pointed to the door. "Right now. Or I will throw you out. And don't ever let me catch you hassling either of them ever again. Got it?"

Jesse's eyes met Sarah's and held them for a second. Then he raised both his hands.

"I'm going." He strode out of the kitchen. Within moments, there was the sound of a truck engine turning over outside. Sarah pushed away from Daniel and dropped into a chair.

"Sarah," Olivia said gently, "none of that was your fault. It's perfectly normal to freeze up or get flustered and not know what to do in a situation like that."

"Jesse wouldn't have hurt me." Sarah crossed her arms. "Not really. He just wanted me to go talk with him somewhere and didn't like that I wouldn't."

"About the money Brian owed him?" Olivia asked. "Or about something else? When I walked in, it looked as though he was trying to kiss you."

"I don't know. It doesn't matter now, does it?" She stared down at the table. The teenager looked angry enough to punch something. But this would hardly be the first time she'd used anger to cover fear.

Daniel sighed. "Olivia's right. This isn't your fault. He laid his hands on you without permission. You can press charges for that."

"No, I won't do it! And if you call the police I won't

cooperate! None of those people you just chased out of here take me seriously as it is!" Sarah's head dropped into her hands. "Everybody thinks I'm some weak, pathetic little kid who can't do anything for herself and has to hide behind *you*. You think it's going to do anything to help my image if word gets out I called the police on Jesse for basically nothing?"

"I understand." Olivia sat down, too. "Your image matters a lot to you, and sometimes people, or even the media, might say things about you that aren't fair. That's going to be a battle you're going to face sometimes. But you can't let that stop you from standing up for yourself."

Sarah's head snapped up. "Do you really think I'm going to listen to you when you're trying to use Daniel and get an article out of me? You think I don't know you have an agenda? I saw you running around outside trying to interview everyone even while Daniel was trying to get them to leave."

Daniel's eyes met Olivia's. "Give us a few moments?"

"Absolutely." Olivia nodded. "But you should both know that before I got through to the police, I got an anonymous threatening phone call on your home line. It sounded like the same guy who tried to kidnap me. Basically just said something like, 'Hey, sunshine, you're not going to get away from me this time.' I told the police."

Daniel sighed heavily. But Sarah didn't even flinch.

"Sarah's been getting a lot of anonymous threats," he said. "It could be one of those."

Or it could be whoever had tried to kidnap Olivia had somehow tracked her down to his house. Either way, he wished she'd told him in private, so he could have decided what and when to tell Sarah. But maybe telling them together was Olivia's way of trying to show Sarah she respected her.

Olivia slipped through the door and out into the night.

"Olivia's right, you know," Daniel said.

Sarah shot him a withering glance that reminded him of Mona. "I don't know who you think you're fooling. You knew I didn't want to be interviewed by a tiny little paper like hers. You only called her because you're attracted to her."

"Not true." Sure, Olivia was an attractive woman. Remarkably so even. Anyone with a pair of eyes in their head could see that. But since he wasn't looking for a relationship, her attractiveness made no difference to him. "I read enough of her stuff to know she's a really good writer. Her newspaper has integrity and she knows a lot about your family's company. Besides, this conversation isn't about her. It's about what just happened between you and Jesse."

"Jesse doesn't matter. He's just some guy who wanted whatever. He isn't important considering everything else going on with Uncle Brian. I should've handled it myself. I shouldn't have asked Olivia to help me make him leave. I never should have involved her in my business, and neither should you!"

Daniel tried to talk things out for a while longer. But after going around the same circles of conversation a few times, he finally wished Sarah good-night and walked outside to find Olivia. His eyes scanned the empty lawn, now marked with tire tracks and the remains of a party that had never really started. Olivia was nowhere to be seen. His feet sped up, taking his heartbeat along with them, as he strode down the driveway, kicking over beer cans and garbage as he went.

Then he noticed the faint glow coming from his workshop and realized the garage door was open a couple of feet. He bent down. "Hey, Olivia? You in there?"

"Yeah. Just checking something."

"What?" He yanked the rolling door up to shoulder level and ducked in.

"Just wanted to make sure no one had done anything to your truck, considering Brian's killers apparently planted some kind of explosives on his car." Her feet stuck out from underneath his tailgate. "But from what I can see, no one's tampered with it." She slid out from under his truck and sat up. "How's Sarah?"

"Defiant." *Same as always.* "She says she doesn't know for sure if Jesse wanted to make a move on her or just talk to her about the company, because all he'd really said was that they should go walk outside and join the party. She told him I was making her stay inside. He grabbed her shoulders, as though he was going to lead her outside or something. That's when you came in. At least, that's her story right now."

"He's a fake," she said. "I didn't buy his phony apology for a second."

"Maybe." He sighed. "Jesse can be pretty charming, but he's always struck me as entitled and a bit too high on himself. Leslie Construction has a pretty rough culture, and Sarah feels as if she has to show everyone she's every bit as tough as Mona. When I became her guardian, she was already smoking, drinking and experimenting with drugs even though she was only fourteen. I did the best I could to keep her from that. But my days of being able to protect her are almost over."

Olivia stood up slowly. "Well, for what it's worth, a girl named Kendra told me the original party invite came from Brian's email address. She figured someone had used his machine for fun, so she passed it on." She ran her hands down her dirty jeans. "What I can't believe is how you got them all to leave. The way you took down Hawk was pretty amazing. I thought you said you weren't a fighter."

"I'm not. You can't control the situation if you can't control yourself." He turned back toward the night, braced his hands on the top of the doorway and looked out. He could practically feel the questions in her eyes boring into his back. "Growing up, I was always taller than all the other kids. Quieter, too. Spent hours alone just building things. Once when I was about twelve, this other kid started picking on me. He was older than me, I think, but smaller. He was pummeling me. Must have hit me eight or nine times." He closed his eyes. "I hit him once. Just once. But it was enough to break his arm in two places."

He heard her cross the room behind him. Her voice was soft. "I'm sorry."

"It's okay." He shrugged but didn't turn. "I started martial arts after that and learned how to protect myself and other people without seriously hurting anyone."

Still, he'd gone and married a woman with no self-control. What a mistake that had been.

He turned back. "Anyway, it's pretty late and apparently there's still heavy rain in the forecast. I was thinking we'd sleep here and drive back to the city first thing tomorrow. I'll take the loft out here. You can have my couch in the study. I know it's not much, but Sarah's already taken the bedroom."

She ran her hand through her wet, sweat-soaked hair. Her clothes were dirty and there was a streak of grease down the side of her face. But somehow she was still so beautiful it took his breath away. By running her hands self-consciously through her hair she only managed to spread the grease farther down her neck. "Actually, I lived out of a suitcase in a whole string of lousy little rented apartments most of my life. By comparison, this place, your home, is really rather wonderful."

She took a step toward him and he felt his chest tighten as if someone had sucked all the air out of the room. How had everything gotten so complicated? Ever since he'd first laid eyes on her in the parking garage it had felt as though they'd both been hurtling from one crisis to another. He'd carried this woman in his arms. He'd cradled her into his chest. But they'd still never shared as much as a cup of coffee together. Yet there was something about being, simply being, in the same airspace as Olivia that made him think that maybe he'd enjoy getting to know her better.

"Everything okay? Daniel? You're staring."

"Sorry. You've just got some grease on you. I've got something for that." He turned away, walked over to his workbench. "You never told me about your call with the police."

"Yeah, Constable Henry of the RCMP." She laughed. "He was very chipper. But his questions were really thorough. Almost felt as if he was investigating me."

Daniel ran his hand over the back of his neck. "I know the feeling. Every cop I've talked to since Brian's initial arrest made me feel as if I was being suspected of something. I can't shake the feeling there's something bigger going on than mere tax evasion. Which is honestly probably another one of the reasons why I thought to call you. I learned overseas that when chaos was breaking out and the authorities were stonewalling, sometimes an honest media source was the best friend you could have."

She leaned back against his truck. A single light bulb suspended from the ceiling cast long shadows down her body, spreading out beneath her feet. "The cops are going to come into the office on Monday to talk to me further, so Vince can sit in. Before you ask, Ricky can meet up with me first thing tomorrow morning to duplicate whatever pictures are on the memory card."

Which I hope means you'll turn the pictures over to the police tomorrow, too. But we can save that argument for later.

He yanked open a drawer and pulled a disposable cleaning cloth from a packet. Then he switched on his workbench lamp. "Come here. There's more light."

She walked over to him and stretched out her hand. He took it and ran his cloth down a long grease smudge on the edge of her wrist until her skin was clean. Then he cupped her face and ran a fresh wipe down her cheek, but the grease stubbornly refused to yield. He pressed harder and leaned in closer, feeling the muscles in her neck tense from the urge to turn her head toward him. His fingertips brushed under her hair. Her eyes closed.

And for the first time in a very long time, he wondered what it would be like to take someone's face in his hands and pull her close, until he felt the warmth of her lips against his. To let himself kiss her, passionately, recklessly, in a way he hadn't kissed anyone since he was a teenager.

He leaped back, wrenching himself free from the feeling like a swimmer escaping the current as it was just about to carry him under.

She opened her eyes. "Did you manage to get it all?"

"Yeah. I did. But you'll want to wash with soap and water before you fall asleep. The cleanser on the wipes is a bit strong." His heart was pounding so hard he was surprised she couldn't hear it.

Lord, help me keep control of my heart.

He dropped the wipe into the garbage. "I'm sorry," he added, "but I think I should probably pop in your office on Monday, too, and have a word with your editor. I'm going to tell him Sarah's decided she doesn't want you covering this story and ask if he can recommend a different reporter, at a different media outlet, we should talk to."

NINE

Daniel's words fell like cement blocks inside the darkened garage.

For a moment, Olivia couldn't believe her ears. "You're going to walk into my boss's office on Monday morning and tell him you want a different media outlet covering this story?"

"It's nothing personal." He didn't even meet her eye. "I think you're a wonderful person and a good reporter. But Sarah's been swamped with media requests. Everyone wants a piece of the teenage heiress from the tragic, disgraced family. They'll exploit her unless she finds the right person to handle her story. I want her to talk to someone who understands where I was coming from, someone on my wavelength."

But I thought I was on your wavelength.

Daniel walked over to the loft and braced his hands on the low loft ceiling. "It's clear Sarah doesn't like you, for whatever reason. Maybe that's my fault. I never brought a woman to the house before, and she seems to think my reasons for calling you are suspect. While I really respect what your newspaper stands for, Sarah's acting like a kid who wanted ice cream and got offered prunes. But from everything I've seen of the newspaper and read about your boss, Vince seems like a good man. He'll be up to speed on all this, thanks to you. Maybe he can help. She'll probably balk less if the suggestion doesn't come from you. Also, I think it's best I leave Sarah out of the request and tell him it's coming from me."

Best? She turned toward the still-open garage door feeling tears of frustration building in the corners of her eyes. He didn't get it. Having a source from an article you're working on walk into your editor's office and say he'd rather trust the story to someone else was pretty much the worst thing someone could do to a reporter. If a journalist couldn't gain a source's trust, they had nothing.

If Daniel told Vince that despite the fact she'd scored exclusive interviews with the Leslie Crew, spent time with him and Sarah and even salvaged photos from the night Brian died, they disliked her so much they wanted the story to go to another newspaper altogether...

Then Vince really would drop her.

And Daniel would be the one who'd hammered the final nail in the coffin.

She blinked hard to keep the tears from falling. *But Daniel doesn't know that Vince is trimming staff. He doesn't even know that saying something like that to Vince could cost me my job.*

She ran both hands hard through her hair and twisted it back at the nape of her neck. She wouldn't tell him. Not now. It would be unprofessional. He was a source, not a friend—no matter how close she might have felt to him sometimes. It wasn't Daniel's job to save her career. Besides, then she'd have to tell him that she'd chased this story entirely on her own, without Vince's blessing or support, and lose whatever remaining respect he had for her.

"Vince is a really good man and he knows a lot of good people in the news industry. I'm sure he can point you in the right direction." She tried to make herself smile, but the best she could manage was not frowning. "Well, I don't know about you, but I'm exhausted. I'll see you tomorrow."

"At least let me walk you back to the house."

"It's forty feet away. I'm sure I'll be fine." She stepped out into the muggy darkness, then paused. "Thank you for everything you've done to try to keep me safe. I really am thankful. I did catch the Morse code warning you tapped on my arm when I was interviewing Hawk." She'd just made the call not to heed it. "Good night, Daniel."

"Sleep well, and don't forget to lock the door behind you."

"I won't." Gravel crunched under her steps. Pale light from the open garage door spread out at her feet. The kitchen was empty. She waved in Daniel's direction, then closed and bolted the door behind her.

She sighed and pulled the notepad out of her back pocket and dropped it on the smooth, polished surface of the reclaimed wood table. Then she fished out the photo memory card and dropped it next to the notepad. She sat down and only then realized that each chair around the table was handcrafted and unique. Her gaze ran to the cabinets. Daniel really was quite the craftsman. Even barely finished, with a foundation pit for a living room and two uninhabitable floors above her, his home really was beautiful.

His home. His life. That she'd accidentally stumbled into without ever having been invited. From his bravery in the face of the jeering thugs in the driveway to his concern for his ward, Sarah, in a few short hours, she'd gotten an up-close, personal, even intimate look into the measure of the man who seemed to have worked so hard at keeping everyone out.

She'd felt so close to him that her eyes had closed and her heart had fluttered when he'd brushed his hand slowly along her cheek back in the garage. But the closeness they shared was an illusion. When he'd scooped her up and run for his truck, it had been because he was a brave and good man. Not because he'd wanted her in his arms. When he'd driven her here, it was because he was doing what it took to get her out of harm's way, not because he was welcoming her into his home. When he'd invited her to spend the night at the house, it was because it was the simplest option logistically, not because he wanted to see her face at this table over morning coffee.

She was still just a suitcase girl who'd landed in another temporary place she didn't actually belong.

"I can give you what you want, you know." A voice came from behind her. "But you have to do something for me."

Olivia spun around. Sarah was standing in the bedroom doorway.

"I'm sorry, I didn't know you were there."

The young woman crossed the floor and stopped on the other side of the table. She looked at Olivia a long moment. Not smiling, not frowning, just looking.

"Look, no hard feelings, all right?" Sarah said. "I know you're a decent writer. I read your stuff when

Daniel gave it to me, and it's not bad. You had my back
when Jesse wouldn't take a hint. You're all right and
I'm sorry if I seemed a bit harsh on you back there."
Sarah's hands gripped the back of a chair. "You just
don't know what it's like to turn on the television and
see your face on every channel, with some terrible old
picture the media took off the internet, or see stupid,
totally wrong articles about you in all the papers with
some line tacked on the end about how you 'refused
to comment.' I just want to take control of my own life
back. Set the record straight."

"I get it." Olivia remembered all too well what it
had felt like to have her own life totally out of her
control. A flush of sympathy filled her heart. "I know
what it's like when other people are making huge decisions for you. I don't blame you for trying to control
what you can."

"Thanks." Sarah ran her fingers through her hair.
"As weird as this sounds, I'm actually kind of protective of Daniel. He was really there for me when I
needed someone. My mom, Mona, she totally did a
number on him. She was the one and only love of his
life. He's never gotten over her. To be honest, I don't
like how you look at him. It's as if you want something from him."

Olivia felt a flush rising to her cheeks. She slid the
photo memory card and notebook back into her pocket
to keep her hands from fidgeting. Had her attraction
to him really been that obvious?

"Anyway." Sarah's arms crossed over her chest.
"I've been thinking about it and I've changed my mind.
I'll do an interview with you. A full, exclusive thing,
and you can run it in the paper right away. Sure, your

paper's small, but it'll get picked up online by other sources, right? At least I know you'll be honest about it and not twist my words around. Plus it will get Daniel off my back and make my life easier. But like I said, you'll have to promise to do something for me."

"Sure. Absolutely. I mean, I'll have to clear it with my editor, Vince, but he's pretty understanding—"

"Not him. You." Her blue eyes fixed on Olivia's face for a long moment. "You have to promise me that after you interview me you will never speak to Daniel ever again."

It was three o'clock in the morning and Olivia couldn't sleep. She rolled over. The sofa creaked beneath her.

Why does it feel that if I agree to Sarah's terms, I'll be making the biggest mistake of my life?

It wasn't as if she and Daniel were friends or had any kind of personal relationship. He'd never given her any indication he planned to keep in touch with her. In fact, he seemed eager to get her out of his life. He wasn't hers to lose.

Yet instead of immediately agreeing to Sarah's terms, she'd just told her she needed to sleep on it. This interview could save Olivia's job and change her life. It would prove she belonged in the *Torchlight* family. It might even give her the stability she needed to stop living in a little apartment and finally buy a place of her own.

What else could possibly matter?

A wool blanket lay over the back of the couch. She pulled it down and draped it over her shoulders. It smelled like Daniel. Every time she tried closing her eyes, his face was there. Dark, soulful eyes, like hot chocolate, mocha and comfort. Gentle lips, curved into a smile. The scruff of his cheek brushing hers.

She got up and got dressed, feeling the memory card and notebook sitting heavy in her jeans' pocket. She left the light off, in case it seeped into Sarah's room, and felt her way along the planks to the front door as her eyes slowly adjusted to the darkness. Then she undid the locks and stepped out onto the front porch. Heavy rain smacked the ground like bullets. Thunder rumbled in the distance. The storm was here and growing worse. She found a corner of the porch where the roof above wasn't leaking and sat down.

Dear God, I know I've said so many times before that I'm done praying to You. But I don't even know what I'm feeling right now and I've got no one else to turn to. Vince always says the only good reason for being awake in the middle of the night is to say those things to You that we're afraid to say in the light of the day. But, basically, I don't know what I believe anymore. About You. About me. About my job. Why I can't ever find a place where I feel like I belong...

She heard the vehicle before she saw it.

A dark van was slowly rolling down the gravel driveway without its headlights on. She pressed her back against the wall. Her heart pounded hard in her chest, sending adrenaline coursing through her veins. In the glow of the running lights, she could see what looked like three figures inside.

The vehicle rolled slowly down the driveway, inching its way up toward her, until it disappeared behind a tree halfway up the driveway. The engine cut. The dim glow of the truck's running lights disappeared. A door slammed. But she couldn't see anyone in the darkness.

She glanced back toward the dark house behind her. Surely Daniel in the garage was too far away to have heard any of that. The vehicle had sneaked up so slowly and quietly that Sarah might have slept through it, too.

She had to warn them.

Olivia slid to her feet and pushed the living room door back open. The hinges creaked loudly. A man's voice shouted from behind her. Her head turned just enough to see a large masked figure running toward her. Faceless and huge. "Hey! You! Stop!"

As though that was going to happen. She slipped into the darkened living room. Her feet scrambled across the maze of boards, feeling her way ahead with each step. First board. Second board. Her steps zig-zagged back and forth across the room.

Heavy feet pounded onto the porch.

Then came the voice—loud, angry and not one she could remember ever hearing before. "I said stop! I'm not supposed to shoot you. But I will if you make me."

Panicked tears flooded her eyes. A still voice inside her mind reminded her that he'd likely kill her even if she cooperated. She forced her feet forward. Just a few more steps and she'd reach where one plank ended and the last board began.

Something metallic clinked in the darkness behind her.

She jumped.

A bullet whizzed through the air. It ricocheted off the wall. Her feet landed in the dark pit beneath the boards. She pitched forward onto her hands and knees into the soft, freshly dug earth. The notepad and memory card fell out of her pocket. She bit her lip and started feeling around for them in the darkness.

The voice above her swore. "I said, don't make me shoot you!"

Her fingers brushed the notepad. She held it in her mouth for a moment and kept searching. She had to find the memory card. If these were the same thugs who killed Brian, the photos on it might be the only clues to who they really were. She felt something crack under her knees. She'd knelt on it but hopefully not destroyed it. She shoved it as far down into her front jeans' pocket as she could and stuffed the notebook in on top of it.

Now to make it out alive.

The doorway loomed above her, a pale gray shape lit by dim light filtering from above the kitchen stove. The planks above her shook. The thug swore.

She crawled forward. There was another click. A flashlight beam struck the wall beside her. She pressed herself into the shadow between the wall and the floor. The light moved back and forth through the room, bouncing off the stone walls, and she could finally get a good look at him.

He was built like a brick wall, in black fatigues and a faceless oval mask, just like the figment from her nightmares and the figure she'd sketched in her notebook. If these men really were the Faceless Crew, then he was definitely the so-called Brute and the one who thought of himself as a weapons expert and assassin.

"You know you can't escape. You're only making things worse for yourself."

A second blast shook the air above her, followed quickly by a third. It was as if he'd lost patience for searching and started firing randomly in an attempt to scare her out. His feet pounded quickly down the boards. His shouts echoed around the room. "Get out here! Now!"

She dropped to her stomach and crawled across the floor toward the open kitchen doorway. Surely Sarah must be awake now, even if the noise probably hadn't carried all the way to Daniel in the garage. But she hadn't seen another person in the kitchen.

Where were the other two men? Had she been wrong to run into the house to try to warn Sarah?

Help me, Lord. I don't know how I'm going to make it out of here alive.

The flashlight beam hit the floor and hovered there. The gunman seemed to have clipped it to his belt. Another bullet landed in the dirt ahead of her. He chuckled and strode down the maze of boards until he hit the start of the final plank, a few feet above her head.

"Give it up, lady!" Another gun blast. Another laugh. "You're trapped. There's no way you're making it out of here alive. I'm just going to keep on shooting and shooting until you're either bleeding or dead."

Well, that might be his plan. But his feet would be wet and slippery from the rain, and the board underneath him was unsteady. She crouched up onto the balls of her feet. Her fingertips pressed into the dirt like a runner. He fired off another bullet. She sprinted underneath the boards.

Her head was low. Her chin was tucked into her chest. She ducked underneath the board he was standing on and ran right underneath his feet. *I'll never complain about being short again.* She could hear him fumbling with his weapon. But it was too late.

Olivia leaped. She pushed up, throwing all her strength into dislodging the board above her head. Her arms ached under his weight.

The board toppled.

The Brute fell.

She hit the doorway and leaped up the wall. Her feet scrambled for grip in the stones as she hauled herself into the kitchen.

"What's happening?" Sarah stood in the bedroom doorway, fully clothed with boots on her feet.

Olivia slammed the living room door behind her. No lock. She shoved a kitchen chair under the handle. "Three men. Look like the ones who killed Brian. At least one has a gun."

Sarah turned and ran back into the bedroom.

"Wait!" Olivia started after her. "We've got to get out of here!"

"That's what I'm doing." Sarah pulled on her raincoat and yanked the window open. Rain whipped in. Thick tree branches brushed inches from the frame. She started to climb through. "You coming, too?"

Olivia shook her head. "I need to warn Daniel."

Sarah paused, sitting with one leg on either side of the window frame. "Okay, tell him that I'm going to run through the woods until I reach the main highway. There's a motel with campgrounds. The one with the creepy clown sign. I'll meet him there."

"That's miles away." And where some of Leslie's crew was headed.

"Yeah, but their office is open all night long, they have a phone and will let me call the police. I know how to get there and it's safer than hiding in the woods waiting for you. Trust me, I used to sneak out there all the time to goof off in their freaky broken fairgrounds." She hopped out the window. "Daniel will totally know where to find me."

She disappeared in the woods without looking back.

Olivia turned and ran through the kitchen toward the back door. Sounded as though the trigger-happy Brute was still trying to make his way out of the living room.

Thank You, Lord, that they didn't get Sarah. Please help me reach Daniel—

The kitchen door flew open before she could even touch her hand to the handle. A tall and unnaturally thin faceless thug leveled the barrel of a gun toward her face.

"Enough games," he said. "You're coming with me."

TEN

It was the rattle of the garage door that first jolted Daniel awake. But it wasn't until his eyes adjusted to the darkness and he saw the outline of a short masked man silhouetted in the faint light that he realized the danger. Daniel silently crept to the edge of the ledge of the loft. He'd been sleeping in the storage area over his workbench, fully clothed, just in case Hawk and his buddies decided to come back.

But this was a threat he hadn't anticipated. This man was a stranger. He was short but hefty, and dressed in dark fatigues and a faceless mask like the men who'd killed Brian in the parking garage. But then he pulled his mask off and stuffed it in a duffel bag. Either he didn't think there'd be anyone in the garage to spot his face or he wasn't planning on leaving any witnesses alive.

Daniel still didn't recognize him.

He couldn't see a weapon in his hand, either, but that didn't mean he wasn't carrying one. For a moment, Daniel almost wished he'd gone into the house and pulled his shotgun from its hiding place. But a hunting firearm like that was hardly intended for close combat.

The man switched on a flashlight. Daniel ducked behind a storage box. The light swung around the room. Over his workbench. Over his truck. Over the battered chair, reading table and camping stove. Up over Daniel's hiding spot in the loft. Then back down again.

Are there more of them? Have they gone into the house? Olivia's computer printout had said the Faceless Crew were a team of three. If so, that would make this small man Shorty, the so-called explosives expert. Getting past this man and rushing into the house would mean giving up the element of surprise, throwing himself into a fight and potentially alerting whoever else was with him.

Lord, help me be wise. Please protect Sarah and Olivia. Keep them safe until I can get to them. Help me know the right way and time to act.

Daniel pressed his fingers against the box directly in front of him. If only he'd come closer, then there were at least half a dozen ways Daniel could think to almost silently take him to the ground without alerting any buddies he might have waiting outside. Shorty set the flashlight down on the ground and pulled something the size of brick from his duffel bag.

A second figure appeared in the doorway. Daniel felt his heart smack so hard against his rib cage he nearly lost his breath.

It was Olivia. She was followed by a thin masked man who could only be described as a "Rake." The masked thug had his hand clamped around Olivia's throat. His other hand pressed a gun to the back of her head.

Daniel's heart lurched with every step she took.

Olivia's hands were tied in front of her. Rainwater streamed down her tiny frame.

Daniel braced his hands on the loft floor and fought the urge to leap. Everything inside him wanted to attack the man gripping her and to fight for her life with every last breath in his body. But if he made a move, the gunman might pull the trigger ending Olivia's life. And he still didn't know if there were more of them or where Sarah was.

His eyes closed for fraction of a second, just long enough to pray.

Oh, God, I have to save her. Help me focus.

The gunman shuffled her across the floor toward the truck. Olivia's eyes didn't even glance toward his hiding spot. But surely she had to know he was there. She had to know he wouldn't just have run off and left her.

Shorty stood up from behind the truck and quickly yanked his mask back on.

"We good?" Rake asked.

"Yup." He wiped his hands on his pants and walked over to the workbench.

Yup. Right this way. Just a little closer...

"What do the three of you want?" Olivia's voice rang loud and clear. "You two, plus that trigger-happy Brute who you left all alone in the house, now trying to figure his way out of the living room."

Oh, she was brilliant! Olivia knew he was there, all right! And in two sentences had managed to give him all the information he needed to assess the situation.

A crew of three faceless thugs. None of whom, it seemed, had Sarah.

"None of your business. Now shut it or I'll gag you." Rake cuffed her in the back of the head with the gun.

Olivia cried out in pain. He opened the passenger door to Daniel's truck. "Get in."

She stepped up onto the running board.

Okay, so his hand is off her throat. The gun will probably slip away from her head for a second or two. Shorty has walked into range. Looks as though this is the best chance I'm going to get. I just need to wait and pick my moment—

Olivia kicked back hard, catching Rake sharply in the gut.

Or she could pick the moment.

Rake collapsed onto the ground and gasped for breath. His gun clattered across the floor. Daniel leaped. He landed on Shorty's shoulders and forced him to the ground. Out of the corner of his eye, he could see a flash of red as Olivia scrambled for Rake's gun.

Daniel leaped to his feet. Shorty's fist caught Daniel in the side of the head. Daniel kicked his legs out from under him.

A gunshot pierced the air.

Olivia screamed. Daniel's heart stopped.

Brute was standing in the garage doorway. His gun was aimed at her face. "Kneel." Olivia knelt. He glanced at the thin man. "Hey, Rake? You mind if I end her now?"

"Hey!" Daniel's hands shot up in the air. "Don't hurt her. Let her go. Whatever you want, you can get from me!"

Shorty laughed.

A swift, hard blow struck Daniel on the back of the head.

The world went black.

ELEVEN

"Daniel! Daniel! Wake up!"

Somewhere in the darkness of Daniel's barely conscious brain, he could hear Olivia shouting like a distant echo coming from the bottom of a tunnel.

"Dear God, please, please help me wake him up! I can't do this alone…"

He heard her praying. But his head ached and he couldn't get his eyes to open. Something was pressing into his forehead. He needed to wake up.

Unconsciousness swept over his mind.

He was passing out again.

A sharp, sudden pain pierced his shoulder.

He jerked awake.

Daniel was half sitting, half lying in the front seat of his truck. They were still in his garage. His wrists were fastened to the steering wheel by plastic zip ties. Long wet hair brushed against his neck. "Ouch! Did you just pinch my shoulder?"

"You're awake!" Olivia kissed his cheek and then she sat back against the passenger seat. Her hands were bound together in front of her. "There's—" Fresh tears choked the words from her lips.

"It's okay. We're in this together. It's going to be okay." Instinctively he found himself wanting to reassure her, even as his mind spun to evaluate the danger he'd just woken up in.

His head ached and he could barely move his hands. But they were still alive, not too badly hurt and still together. "Where are they?"

"Heading down the driveway. Haven't heard them drive off yet."

"Where's Sarah?"

"She managed to escape into the woods. She said she'd meet you at the motel on the highway."

Thank You, God.

"That's a relief. Are you able to get the glove compartment open? I stashed a really good, sharp knife in there before I went to bed. Should be able to cut through these ties."

Her eyes darted to the glove compartment. "I'm pretty sure there's a bomb in here with us somewhere. Rake asked Shorty how long they had before the truck exploded. I was afraid to touch anything or try to open the door in case that's what set it off."

Just like that, the bit of relief he'd felt turned to a cold and focused fear. "How long ago did they leave?"

"Couple minutes. Not long. All I know is it's a bigger bomb than the one that took out Brian's car, so this time they went for a timer instead of a remote, because Shorty was worried about getting far enough away."

"You keep using the same code names as the Faceless Crew website. Why?"

"That's what they kept calling each other."

"Okay. Well, if you didn't hear them pelt down the driveway and peel out of here, then we probably have a few minutes." But probably not much more than that. "I watched Shorty mess with the back of the truck. Pretty sure he didn't go anywhere near the cab."

She opened the glove compartment and pulled out a retractable utility knife. She slid the blade out with her fingertips.

Daniel pulled his hands as far away from the steering wheel as he could. There was less than an inch of cutting space between the cuffs and his skin. "You want me to talk you through it?"

"No. Just keep quiet and don't move."

Her hands brushed his. The knife slid past his wrists. She cut him free. A vehicle engine roared in the night air. He took the knife, grabbed Olivia's fingers and set her wrists loose. "Come on."

They leaped from the truck and slid through the gap under the garage door out into the rain. He grabbed her hand and pulled her into the trees. They ran through the woods, stumbling over underbrush, pushing through the branches. "Thank You, God, that we—"

An explosion shook the air. Heat surged toward them. Smoke billowed through the trees behind them. Red-and-orange flames flickered in the sky. The smell of burning wood filled his lungs. A cry escaped Olivia's lips. Pain filled her eyes.

"It's just a building." His hand tightened in hers. "Come on. We've got to keep running."

She squeezed back. They ran for as long as their bodies could take it. Rain blurred their vision. His lungs ached. But it wasn't until he heard Olivia panting for breath that he slowed his pace to walking. "You said Sarah's heading to the clown motel?"

She gasped in a long breath. It sounded painful.

"Yeah. She said she'd call the police from there. I know that's where the Leslie crew was planning to party, but she said it was the safest place to go."

"Maybe she's right. At least she got away." He'd have preferred she'd stayed close by and waited to run with them. But there was nothing to be done about it now. "She always loved that place. I don't know what it is with teenagers and wanting to sneak into broken fairgrounds."

The rain grew heavier. Lightning split the sky. He glanced at Olivia. She was soaked, her clothes were streaked with dirt and he could feel her shivering through their joined hands. Yet somehow she was still holding her head high. He'd never seen someone look so fragile and yet so strong at the same time. He wished he had something to offer her other than the thin, soaked T-shirt on his back. Olivia pulled out her cell phone, cupped it under her arm and checked for a signal. It was only then he realized they were still holding hands.

"Got a signal?"

"No." She slid her phone back into her pocket. "And my phone's not waterproof, so I want to keep it in my pocket."

"I've still got my wallet on me." Plus the knife from the glove compartment. "You?"

She nodded. "My wallet. My notepad and the photo memory card."

Well, that was something. But for now they were alone. In the woods. With not much more than the clothes on their backs. And each other.

And You, Lord. Thank You for helping us get out of there alive.

They kept walking. He told Olivia that he'd seen Shorty's face, but hadn't recognized him as anyone from either the Leslie Construction crew or the trial. Olivia told him about Brute chasing her through the living room. He nearly whistled. Her bravery was astounding.

"After you were knocked out, I went limp," she said. "Figured it was best to save my strength, at least as long as they were keeping us together. They thought I'd fainted and started talking a bit more freely then. From what I was able to piece together, they were hired by someone who didn't just want Brian dead, but wanted to make an impressive, showy statement of killing him. Which isn't that far off what we suspected already. Shorty was worried 'the client' was going to be angry that the explosion might not be big enough to demolish the house, too, because the rain would keep the fire from spreading, and apparently the client wanted both your vehicle and house destroyed—"

"What?" His voice rose sharply. "The client wanted them to demolish my house? Why?"

Whoever had hired the Faceless Crew hated the Leslies so much they actually wanted to blow up the house he was restoring?

"I don't know. But I do know that using bombs and explosives matters to them. Rake yelled at Brute for shooting his gun off at me, because no one would take them seriously as a gang if they didn't stick to the pattern of people dying in explosions, and that's why the client had hired them. He added it didn't matter if they hated him or not, because the client was on the fast track to heading up something big. I don't know what that means."

"Neither do I." But he didn't like the sound of it. "In my experience, bombs are an intimidation tactic used by people who want to prove they're scary. Making a big, flashy show of it like that just makes your job harder." And destroying a whole house was definitely an escalation over a simple car bomb.

"Rake was plenty mad at both of them." She smacked a branch out of her face. "He said the client might even make them go back and blow up your house. Sorry."

"It's okay." The forest floor grew wetter until they were trudging through water up to their ankles. Now the rain was beating so hard he could barely see. More lightning, this time forked and dangerous. He slid his arm around her shoulder and shifted course. "Weather's getting worse. We're not safe out here. I think we should take shelter until there's a break in the storm, or at least until the lightning stops. There's a tiny ghost town north of us. Just a handful of empty buildings and two stop signs. But there should still be something there with a roof."

Thunder rumbled above them. Another flash of lightning.

They started running.

TWELVE

The trees parted. A narrow and twisted back road lay at their feet. Water coursed down it like a river. They sloshed in. Daniel grabbed Olivia's hand. The water was already knee-deep on her.

Rain beat against their bodies as though it was trying to push its way straight through. Branches and debris swirled down the water past them. Southern Ontario was no stranger to harsh late-summer thunderstorms, but he couldn't remember the last time he'd seen a storm hit this hard. If the rain didn't let up soon, a lot of the roads would be impassable. And even more rain was predicted to fall before the weekend was through.

The dark, ghostly shapes of abandoned stores and houses appeared ahead of them in the gloom. A small brick church sat by the edge of town. He pulled Olivia toward it. The door was closed, but it opened when he leaned his shoulder into it. They tumbled out of the rain. Olivia held up her cell phone and shone the light over the abandoned space. A couple of broken pews. A few dusty crates of books. An old hand-drawn sign announcing a strawberry social that had no doubt been held a very long time ago. She switched the phone off and slid it back into her pocket. "I still can't get a signal and the battery is down to five percent."

"I wouldn't be surprised if the storm knocked out the cell towers."

Maybe even the electricity and phones, too. Thankfully, Sarah had escaped before the worst of the storm hit. Hopefully she was safe at the motel now, curled up in the shabby front lounge chatting with the police. Olivia sat on the floor and looked out at the rain. He sat beside her. The motel and campgrounds were probably less than an hour's walk now. Rain like this came in waves. They'd wait for the next break then start running again.

"I never realized just how many abandoned buildings there were out in the country." A sad sigh left Olivia's body. "I can't imagine having a home and just leaving it."

Yeah, he'd felt similarly the first time he'd realized such a picturesque world existed commuting distance from Toronto. "Well, a lot of smaller farms and communities are struggling economically. Factories and farms shut down. Stores can't afford to keep their doors open. Towns die. People leave. Sometimes shutting the door and walking away is easier than fighting for something that no longer seems livable." He shook his head. "But I was hoping that one day I'd move up here permanently."

Olivia pressed her lips together. The soft patter of rain and rumble of thunder filled a long pause between them.

"I never had a home," she said. "We moved constantly when I was growing up, all over Canada and the States.

So I lived in a lot of temporary apartments. Nineteen total by the time I left for college. Sometimes I'd just get settled in a school, then wake up the next day to hear we were moving again. Sometimes I'd just have an air mattress and a suitcase on the floor. Everything I owned fit in one big red suitcase."

"I'm sorry," he said. "I definitely know what it's like to live out of a suitcase. But it's different when you're an adult and choose it."

"Well, my dad was in manufacturing and had trouble keeping steady work. He was definitely in a tough segment of the industry and there weren't a lot of jobs going. But he had a lot of conflicts with employers, too. Some refused to pay him his final paycheck or paid him less than he thought he was owed. Which is why I took the Leslie Construction trial and the idea Brian cheated all those people kind of personally at first. Dad blames everyone but himself. Mom definitely blames him. They barely managed to stick together while I was young, and eventually split up when I left home. My sister, Chloe, blames both of them." She leaned against his shoulder.

"Blame's a tricky thing." He slipped his arm around her. "At least for me anyway. Don't always know where to put it, and sometimes it's hard to get rid of the need to. For a long time I blamed Mona, one hundred percent, for ruining our marriage by cheating on me and leaving. Not to mention blaming her for her drug and alcohol problems. Because, obviously, those were her choices." He could feel Olivia's hair against his cheek. He ran his hand down over her shoulder until his fingers brushed against her hand. "I blamed Rita, too, for taking her in when she left me and encouraging her in her dangerous lifestyle. But, in the end, I also blame myself for not seeing it coming. See, my parents got married as teenagers and were together their whole lives. Mona was the first time I'd ever fallen in love. I just took it for granted that it was all going to work out for us the way it did for my parents."

He hadn't thought it through. He hadn't gone into his marriage with his eyes open. He'd been too swept up in emotion. He couldn't ever let that happen again.

"I blamed God," Olivia said. "My mom used to take me to church with her and I loved it. Because it didn't matter whether we were in Manitoba or Florida, there were people who all sang the same songs, read the same Bible stories and welcomed me like family. I used to pray every single time we moved that this move would be the last, that this time I'd finally have a real house of my own, that this time God would keep my dad from fighting with people. Eventually, I got so hurt and angry, I stopped praying..."

Her voice trailed off into sob. He pulled back just enough to turn and face her. "Hey, it's okay."

She shook her head. "No, it's not. Because I got so caught up in trying to protect my job with the paper that I wasn't fully honest with you. I never lied to you. But I also never told you that Vince was cutting staff. I never told you that I needed this Leslie Construction story to keep my job. I never told you that Vince doesn't know I'm up here chasing this story and in fact told me not to chase it—"

What? Frustration rose at the back of his neck. He could feel his shoulders stiffen and pull back, in that old familiar way they'd done every time he'd caught

Mona lying to him. He started to pull away. Then stopped.

There were tears building in the corners of Olivia's eyes.

"I don't have a home." Tears flooded her voice, too. "Just a small apartment. I haven't even bought curtains or shelves to decorate it because I live every day half expecting that something's going to happen and I'll need to move on. My mom, dad and Chloe all live in completely different places. *Torchlight* was the closest thing I had to somewhere I belonged and I chased this story hard because I didn't want to lose that."

He stopped himself from pulling away and felt her head fall into the crook of his neck.

"I always feel as though I'm clinging on so tight to everything because I'm afraid something's going to take it away from me," she said. "It's exhausting. But spending time with you, seeing how you treat people, hearing how you just pray as if talking to God is as normal as breathing, reminds me of how much I miss having faith in something bigger than myself. You made me realize I miss praying. You made me realize I hate what it feels like to not trust anyone or anything. You're such a good man, Daniel. You don't disrespect Mona's memory, even though she treated you badly. You take great care of Sarah, even when she pushes you away. You were even decent to Hawk and Rita and Jesse and Trent. You've been good to me. Even though I'm just some totally unwelcome, unwanted intrusion that tumbled into your life—"

Tears choked out her words.

"Hey! Listen to me." He took her face in both hands. "I'm not going to pretend I'm happy that you came up here without telling your editor." In fact, the tension in the back of his neck told him he'd probably need a bit of time to process out how he felt about it. "But you're being way too hard on yourself. We all do lousy things. We all have moments we regret. Sometimes it feels as though I've more than used up my quota of forgiveness and second chances."

His fingertips brushed the sides of her face. Her eyes were locked on his face. Even battered and exhausted, she was breathtaking. His voice grew husky. "And yeah, you kind of unexpectedly fell into my life, Olivia. But no, trust me, you're not unwanted or an intrusion. Believe it or not, I actually really like having you around. I'm glad we're in this together."

"Thank you." She smiled, a soft, gentle smile that set her eyes dancing. "I'm glad we're in this together, too."

The corners of his lips turned up into a wry smile. His fingers slid up into her tangled hair. She was so close he could feel her breath on his skin. He pulled her closer still and a thought crossed his mind that made his heart stutter a beat—

He'd never felt someone fit so comfortably and simply between his arms before.

Her head tilted toward his. His mouth brushed over hers. He let himself kiss her. Gently. Sweetly. With a tenderness he'd never felt before.

But their lips had barely met when she pushed him back hard.

"I'm sorry! I can't!"

He let her go, feeling both stunned and embarrassed. Not to mention angry at himself. "Then, I'm sorry, too."

"No, you don't understand." Olivia leaped to her

feet. "Sarah told me she'd give me an exclusive interview on the condition I promised to stay away from you. And I didn't say no."

She watched as he frowned and the light dimmed from his eyes. Realizing she'd hurt him felt worse than anything he could have said. She turned away and let the drizzle outside fill her view.

I didn't say yes to Sarah, either! I didn't say anything. But I definitely considered saying yes. He deserved to know.

After all, what would happen when they showed up together at the motel and met up with Sarah? After hugs of relief and police reports, then what? They'd probably all be right back where they'd started. Olivia would still need a story to keep her job. Daniel would be more convinced than ever that it was best to find another reporter. The young, self-centered heiress would probably yet again force Olivia to choose between the job that she loved and the fledgling feelings she'd felt when Daniel's lips met hers.

"Looks as though the rain's let up for now." Daniel stood up. "We should go. There's no way of knowing when the next break in the rain will be, and I don't want to get stuck out here all night."

His voice was pleasant enough. He was back to using that same charming yet totally guarded tone he'd used when they'd first met up in the diner, for a coffee they'd never actually managed to have. As if they were now nothing but acquaintances again.

Maybe that was all they ever were.

"Good idea." She didn't meet his eye.

They stepped back out into the night and kept running, faster this time, as if they were both trying to hurry away from the moment of closeness they'd barely shared. He jogged ahead of her, casting occasional glances back to make sure she was still following. They stuck to the sidewalk until it disappeared and then ran along what would have been the shoulder. The rain had tapered, but water still coursed down the road. The news had reported that even more rain would fall by the time the weekend was through.

They climbed a hill. Faint lights of highway and the motel lay in the distance ahead. She breathed a sigh of relief. They trudged down, side by side, through the damp, dark air.

"The photographer who drove you up is named Ricky, right?" Daniel asked. "Do you trust him?"

She blinked. It felt like ages since either of them had said anything. "Yeah, he's a really good guy. Why?"

"Who else knew you were coming up here?"

"Just Ricky. Again, why?"

Tension rose up her back. She couldn't read his face in the darkness. But his voice was so calm and logical, it almost sounded cold.

"Because someone tried to kidnap you outside the diner," he said. "Because someone brought trouble and violence to my house in the night. I let it go the first time you told me your friend from work couldn't be involved. But now that I know you came up on your own without going through the proper channels, I'm beginning to think it's even more possible the trouble came from someone on your end."

Her jaw dropped and for a moment she couldn't even think of what to say. "You can't be serious."

"Oh, I'm deadly serious." Now his voice had a bitter edge. "I've been doing nothing but thinking for the past while. All I can think is someone took a picture of us outside the diner and we still don't know why someone would do that."

"Yeah, but that wasn't actually Ricky. You just thought it was. Remember? I found out he hadn't made it back yet—"

He kept talking as though she hadn't even spoken. "And then someone tried to kidnap you."

"Yes, someone with a mask just like the three men who killed Brian and just torched your garage."

"Yes. But he didn't look like Rake, Brute or Shorty to me. His mask was similar but less distinctive."

Yeah, she'd come to the same conclusion when talking with Ricky. None of the men who'd just blown up Daniel's garage had the same gravelly voice that had taunted her in the car and on the phone.

"So maybe my abductor was the client who hired them. Or maybe he's a fourth member of the Crew, and there are more Faceless men out there than we knew about. I don't know. I just know that none of what we're going through has to do with me or my paper."

Why were they even fighting about this?

"How can you be so sure?" He let out a sigh that was so gruff it almost sounded like a growl. "We suspect all the trouble we've been in is connected to Brian, because he was a lying, stealing lowlife. I just took it for granted that someone tried to abduct you because of your connection to me. I even wondered if someone mistook you for Sarah in the darkness. You probably have wondered the same thing. But how can you be so sure that your own reckless, impulsive tendencies to just *do* things without thinking haven't been putting us in trouble?"

Because I'm not your former wife! I might be a bit impulsive, I might have interviewed those construction workers instead of hiding in the house as instructed, but I don't consort with criminals!

The words crossed her mind, but she bit them back before they left her lips. He was obviously hurting. His life had been threatened. His truck and garage had exploded. It would be totally understandable if he was having trouble processing everything that had happened. The least she could do was take a turn being the calmer one.

"I'm sorry that you're upset," she said. "I'm really sorry for my part in that. I'm not proud of how I've handled everything. But rather than suspecting my friend, isn't it a lot more likely that whoever killed Brian wants to hurt you and Sarah, too? Maybe someone he stole from is out for payback?"

"Yes, but hiring killers takes money. Nobody working construction is going to have the cash just lying around to hire a gang of thugs. A lot of them were living paycheck to paycheck as it was, even before Brian stopped paying them."

Yes, but it's not as if a newspaper photographer is going to have that kind of money, either. And that's assuming he'd have any reason to attack us.

"It's not that I don't think several of them would have quite happily hurt Brian or even taken his life," Daniel added. "But they'd just grab a baseball bat and take matters into their own hands. What I don't understand is how hiring thugs with weapons and explosives fit in, even if they're just low-level thugs. Because normal people don't hire gangs. They don't know how or even where to start. It's more likely their client himself has gang ties."

Good point. "I heard both Hawk and Rita have criminal records. Maybe they spent time in prison and made friends?"

"Yes, but it's not likely. We're talking the kind of drinking and assault charges where they pled guilty and got probation. It's not as though they served long stints in the kind of high-security prisons that would house murderers and lethal arsonists."

"What about Trent? He carried himself like a man who was capable of doing serious damage if he wanted to, and nobody knew much about him." She was slipping into reporter mode now, but at least they were talking.

"Maybe," Daniel said. "He's definitely a dark horse that one."

"Okay, and what about the police?"

"What about them?"

"Well, Ricky says the only reason he didn't come back sooner, besides getting lost, is some cop sent him on a crazy detour. Some cop also harassed me at the courthouse just before Brian died, and he covered his badge number so I couldn't report him. You've said all along that the cops haven't been straight with you and you felt they're treating you like a suspect. For that matter, my conversation with Constable Henry felt kind of off, too. So maybe we should consider there's something dirty going on with the cops?"

Something else was niggling at the back of her mind. Something involving cops. But she couldn't put a finger on it. She just wished she could talk to her sister. The insight of a detective would come in pretty handy right about now. Not to mention some sisterly support and understanding. While she hadn't taken Chloe's warnings seriously at first, maybe there'd been a good reason she'd told her to drop the story. But even her sister didn't know she was up here with Daniel.

The ground leveled off beneath their feet, thankfully on higher ground than before, because now the water was barely over the soles of her shoes. Daniel fell silent. They trudged on and finally passed the boarded-up entrance to the remains of the shabby fairgrounds and playground. Next came a very long wooded lot. Scattered trailers and tents lay half-hidden behind the trees, barely illuminated by a handful of dimly glowing lampposts. If anyone from the Leslie Construction crew had moved their party here, they'd either moved it inside or given up and gone to sleep. It couldn't be that many hours now until the morning. Finally, Olivia and Daniel crossed the tarmac. The shabby clown sign leered down at them.

The motel was a long brown building, two stories tall. Only a handful of the lights seemed to be working. A sagging balcony ran along the second floor. A man and a woman stood on it, leaning up against the warped and rusted railing. Their heads were bent together—they seemed to be staring down at where raindrops hit the yellow-green water of the algae-filled pool.

Olivia looked at the tops of their heads as she passed. The man had dark hair and a short-sleeved T-shirt stretched tight over his muscles. She tapped Daniel's arm. "Isn't that Trent?"

He grimaced. "I'm afraid so."

So it looked as though at least one of the Leslie

Construction team members whom Daniel had tossed off his property had made it here to the motel and RV park. Hopefully he wasn't about to start something. Olivia didn't know where she recognized the woman from though. She was tall, with long platinum blonde hair, jean shorts and cowboy boots. The blonde whispered something in Trent's ear.

"How about her?" Olivia's voice dropped. "She looks familiar, but I can't place her."

"I don't know her," Daniel said. "She's not on the crew, and I don't remember seeing her back at the house." They stepped out of the rain and under the main office awning. "Now, I'm just going to run in and see about Sarah. You okay waiting for me for a second out here?"

Yeah, probably best they didn't greet Sarah together. She and Daniel were bound to need a few minutes alone. Whatever Daniel decided to say to Sarah about the fact she'd offered Olivia an interview in exchange for walking out of his life for good, she was sure it wouldn't be the easiest conversation.

There was a bench right by the front door. She sat. "No problem. I'll be right here if you need me."

"Thank you." He smiled. His eyes met hers, and for a second, she thought she caught a small echo of the same sweet tenderness that had filled his gaze back in the abandoned church. Then he rubbed his hand over his face and the look was gone. "Once I sort out Sarah, I'll see if we can each book rooms, even just to have a quick nap in. It doesn't look as though the cops have gotten here yet. Back in a second."

She turned her back from the office and watched the rain for a moment. Her tired eyes closed. *Lord, I'm too exhausted and sore right now to even know what to pray, besides to say I'm sorry I haven't trusted You in the past and thank You that we made it this far.*

The office door flew open so hard the screen crashed against the wall. She leaped to her feet. Daniel rushed out and started toward the pool.

"Hey!" She grabbed his arm. "Where's Sarah? Is she okay? Did she call the police?"

Anger burned in Daniel's eyes. "The good news is that according to the motel manager she made it here about an hour ago just fine. But she didn't manage to call 9-1-1 because their phones are dead. Most likely the phone lines went down in the storm. Their power's down, too, so they're on a backup generator. He offered her a room for the night. But she said she'd rather bunk in Rita's motor home."

Okay, only Daniel's feet were still moving, dragging them both in the opposite direction of the campgrounds. Her hand tightened on his biceps. "At least we know she's okay, right?"

Rita might not be his favorite person, but if he was just annoyed then she'd have expected a loud sigh at the news. Instead, Daniel looked ready to blow.

"Manager said he would've walked her to the RV park, but some big dark-haired guy in a muscle shirt pulled her aside and they started arguing about something—"

Uh-oh.

"—and his tall platinum blonde girlfriend jumped in the fight."

THIRTEEN

Daniel glanced up. Trent and the platinum blonde were still standing on the concrete balcony just over the pool. He started for the stairs.

"How could the motel manager just let a teenager get bullied by strangers?" Olivia was at his side.

"He didn't know her age and he figured the platinum blonde was Rita."

As much as he wanted to pelt up the stairs, taking them three at a time, he forced himself to walk. He didn't want to fight. But when they hit the top of the flight and turned toward the pair, the platinum blonde glanced their way, tossed one hand in what almost looked like a dismissive wave, then took off down the landing. Trent scowled and started toward them.

Daniel turned to Olivia. "Just go back to the bottom of the stairs, wait there and stay out of harm's way."

"No. You talk to Trent. I'll follow the blonde."

Olivia only managed four steps before Trent's arm shot out, blocking her path. "Where do you think you're going?"

Olivia pointed over his shoulder. "I'm going to talk to your friend there."

Trent's jaw set firmly. "I don't know what kind of business you think you have with my lady, but no you're not."

"How about the business that you were both seen fighting with Sarah?" In two strides Daniel had caught up to them. "Now, where is she?"

Trent shrugged. "I don't know. That kid's your business, not mine."

Not good enough. Trent might be new to the construction crew, but he'd definitely been there long enough to be owed money, especially if Olivia's research was correct and Trent had never worked on the books. The platinum blonde disappeared through a motel room door. That had better not be where Sarah was.

Olivia glanced back quickly at Daniel. "I really need to go talk to that woman. It's important."

In other words, Olivia recognized her from somewhere and wanted to run off and interview her. Her hand brushed his arm. Her fingers tapped gently on his skin. He pulled away. No, she didn't get to try to use his own Morse code signal to chase down an interview.

"No," he said firmly. "You don't. You need to trust me. You need to switch off your reporter brain and not run around trying to interview people when there are more important things going on. I don't have the energy for arguing with you and Trent at the same time."

Especially now that he'd noticed the telltale bulge of a no doubt illegal handgun inside the cuff of Trent's jeans. Olivia had no idea how much danger she was potentially in right now, and she wouldn't stand still long enough for him to warn her.

"You don't understand." Fierce determination

flashed in her eyes. "Trust me. It is important. I know who she is—"

"I don't care!" Daniel's voice rose. He hated that he'd just cut her off, but didn't know how else to get through to her. Couldn't she tell he was trying to de-escalate the situation? All she was going to do was ramp it up. "I don't care who you think she is or how you think she's connected to the Leslie Construction guys colluding with Brian's theft, or the Faceless Crew or who did what at the courthouse. You need to stop trying to interview people. You need to stop trying to get the news story. You need to stop running into danger."

The intensity in her eyes focused with the control of a laser. "And how much would you know about *any* of that if it hadn't been for my investigating?"

"Girl, listen to your man," Trent said.

"He's not my man," Olivia said, "and I'm done listening."

"Well, then, listen to me," Trent said firmly, "and leave well enough alone." He grabbed Olivia's arm and pulled her back hard.

Daniel broke Trent's hold on Olivia and spun him around. "I really don't want to fight you. But if you ever touch Olivia again, I will take you out."

Olivia slipped past them and dashed down the landing. Before either man could stop her, she reached the motel door that the tall blonde had disappeared through. She knocked three times on the door, then she cupped her hands to the window and looked inside.

"Can you see Sarah?" Daniel called. "Is she in there?"

The motel door flew open. In one swift motion, the blonde wrapped one arm around Olivia's throat. A gun flashed in the other hand, pointed toward Daniel as if in a threat not to follow. A moment later, she dragged Olivia backward into the motel room. The door slammed shut behind them.

The whole thing had happened in seconds.

Fire surged through Daniel's veins so quickly he actually saw red.

Suddenly, it was as if everything he knew about calming a volatile situation and de-escalation had evaporated from his mind.

Olivia was locked in a motel room with someone brandishing a weapon.

He had to save her. Nothing else mattered.

"Get out of my way, Trent, or I'll be forced to hit you."

"Back off, Daniel. Take a walk. Olivia's going to be just fine. This isn't your fight."

"Yeah, it is." With one swift kick, Daniel sent Trent stumbling forward. He expected Trent to fall. But his opponent was stronger than he'd realized and managed to regain his footing.

Trent spun back. His hands raised in a grappling stance. "Look, I told Olivia to leave it alone. But she didn't listen. So now the women are just going to have to sit down together and have a nice, quiet talk."

As if I believe that. Daniel swung, aiming the punch right at his face.

Trent stepped to the side and blocked the shot. He grabbed the pressure point on Daniel's arm, sending blinding pain shooting through his limbs.

The pain woke him up hard and snapped his brain to attention. How was he suddenly being outmatched? He'd lost focus. He was fighting hot and forgetting everything he knew about staying in control in a fight. *I'm emotionally compromised and acting like a street punk. I need to be smarter than this.*

Daniel relaxed his muscles.

Trent loosened his grip. "Look, man, back off. I promise I'm not going to rough her up. Just go find Sarah. She's probably with Hawk and Rita."

"Sorry." Daniel took three steps back. "But I'm not going anywhere without Olivia."

He charged, caught Trent hard in the stomach and knocked him backward. Trent roared. He raised his hand to strike. But Daniel didn't give him a chance. He grabbed Trent's arm and spun him against the rusted metal railing.

The railing broke.

Trent fell backward off the balcony.

His hand grabbed Daniel's shirt. Daniel wrenched himself free.

But it was too late. Daniel lost his balance and fell after him.

Both men hit the pool.

Daniel landed on top of Trent, pushed away and swam hard for the poolside. Rain beat his body. The tiles were slick with algae but Daniel managed to hop onto the deck. Trent grabbed his ankle. He kicked back hard and caught Trent in the shoulder. Trent let go.

Daniel sprinted for the stairs.

"Olivia!" He pounded on the motel room door with both hands. "Are you okay? Whoever's in there, you'd better open this door. Let. Olivia. Out. Now."

No answer. The curtains covering the sole window were closed. Beneath him, he could see Trent standing on the pool deck. He pulled a gun from his ankle holster. Daniel was done knocking.

"Get back from the door!" He leveled one swift kick at the center of the door. It flew open.

The blonde was standing alone in the living room area of a dingy motel suite. Behind her, the door leading to the adjoining room lay open. She aimed the handgun at his head. "Get out. Now."

"I'll die before I let you kill Olivia." He dived underneath the weapon, expecting her to shoot and hopefully miss. But the gun didn't go off. He forced her arms above her head and wrenched the weapon from her hands. "Look, I don't want to hurt you, but you need me to tell me where Olivia is."

"Daniel! It's okay. I'm here." Olivia stepped through from the next room. A huge black sweatshirt now fell over her tiny frame like a dress. "You can drop the gun."

Daniel stepped back from the blonde. But he kept her weapon held tight in his grip. "Not until I know what's going on here."

"Don't tell him." The blonde's green eyes shot a warning across the room.

"Sorry, I won't lie to him. Daniel and I have been through way too much together." She stepped toward them. "Daniel, that's my older sister, Chloe."

Her sister? He stepped back. The hand holding the gun fell to his side. His gaze ran from one sister to the other. Chloe was a good foot taller than Olivia with strong shoulders and an athletic build. Yet the scowls on their pursed lips and the frustrated gazes they now fixed on each other were identical. "You told me she's a cop."

"She is." Olivia sat down. "I haven't seen her in months. I didn't know what the story was with her and Trent, and I didn't want to say anything in front of him, in case he didn't know she was a cop. When she recognized me, she signaled at me to follow her. That's why I was tapping on your arm, trying to get you to listen to me."

"Detective Sergeant Chloe Brant. Ontario Provincial Police." Chloe stretched out a hand toward Daniel. Her voice was exhausted but her handshake was still firm. "I'm not here officially. I'm just visiting someone. But I still didn't want Olivia letting anyone know I was a cop. Up until five minutes ago I didn't even know my little sister knew you personally, and my priority was to get her away from you. The gun was intended to dissuade you from following her and encourage you to take a walk. But Olivia tells me I was very badly misinformed about you."

That was putting it mildly. How could anyone who knew him at all think that seeing Olivia yanked into a motel room by someone with a gun would result in anything but him moving heaven and earth to come after her? Something was very wrong here. "The motel manager said you were fighting with Sarah."

"Sort of. Trent and I were trying to figure out why she'd just arrived here alone in the middle of the night. She wouldn't tell us. It got a bit heated. But she's here and she's safe. We followed her to Rita's trailer and watched her go inside. Last I heard, Rita was going to let her try to make a phone call on her cell, and then sleep there for a bit."

Thank You, God, for that. The digital clock wasn't working, but the round plastic one on the wall said it was almost five o'clock. Police would have almost definitely been dispatched, considering she was a minor reporting a violent crime in progress. Probably wasn't a bad idea to let her nap at Rita's for a tiny bit longer. Rita might be plenty rough around the edges, but she genuinely cared about Sarah. Sarah would have to wake up for the cops soon enough.

Chloe ran her fingers through her unnaturally blond hair. It was a wig. "Daniel, again, I'm sorry for the misunderstanding. Now, if you don't mind, I'd appreciate it very much if you could leave my sister and me to have our talk. Please don't tell anyone that I was here. I'll take care of Olivia from here and make sure she gets home safely. Please respect our privacy and don't contact my sister again."

"No." Olivia stood up. "You don't get to tell Daniel to leave. I don't care what you've been told about Daniel or what you think you know. You're wrong about him." She looked up at Daniel. "Chloe took desperate action to drag me away from you because she thought my life was in danger from you. Somebody, somewhere, thinks you're the bad guy. Turns out you're the prime suspect in Brian Leslie's murder."

Chloe winced. "I wish you hadn't told him that."

"I'm sorry, but treating Daniel like a suspect instead of somebody who could actually help in the investigation will just put more people in danger." Olivia crossed her arms in front of her chest. "The idea Daniel could be guilty of anything like that is so wrong it's laughable. I trust him with my life. We *saved* each other's lives just a few hours ago. The Faceless Crew held us both at gunpoint and torched his garage."

Daniel felt the blood leave his face. He was the prime suspect in Brian's death?

But the shock he felt was nothing compared to how pale Chloe's face was. "The Faceless Crew targeted Daniel and tried to murder him? Are you sure?"

"Positive." Olivia's voice dropped softly. She squeezed her sister's arm gently. "They've been after us both. The good news is that Daniel saw one of their faces. So please, Chlo, tell whoever decided Daniel's a killer that they're very wrong. They need to stop treating him like a suspect and start cooperating with him."

"Down on the floor! Hands behind your head!" Trent burst through the doorway. He was soaking wet. One hand clenched a gun. The other held a badge. "I'm Constable Trent Henry of the RCMP. You're under arrest."

Heat rose to the back of Daniel's neck. He should have realized Trent was a cop. All those years he'd spent watching people, learning to read people, and somehow he'd missed something this important. Worse yet, he'd lost his cool and launched into a fight with the man. He'd tossed a cop off a motel balcony and into a pool.

All because he'd thought Olivia had been in danger.

"I said, get down on the ground." Trent dropped the badge, but the gun was still aimed right at them.

Daniel stepped in front of Olivia and felt her fingers brush his back.

"Put the gun down, Trent." Chloe stood up. "That's my little sister you're pointing it at."

"I'm not arresting her." Trent kicked the door shut behind him. It was cracked and splintered around the lock, but still managed to close. He stepped into the room. "But I'm putting Daniel Ash under arrest for assault. He's finally slipped up and given me a reason to bring him in. He escalated things into a physical fight when all I was trying to do was restrain him."

"You know full well it looked as though Olivia was in danger and I didn't know you or Chloe were cops." Daniel kept his hands down by his sides. Chloe's gun stayed firm in his grasp. "Just let me go check on Sarah and make sure she's okay. She's my responsibility. I'm not going anywhere without her."

"You're not going anywhere at all." Trent nodded at Chloe. "Get my handcuffs from my bag."

The cop was holding his gun in his left hand. Strange, considering he'd definitely fought like a right-handed man. His right arm now lay limp at his side, and even through his shirt Daniel could see his shoulder bone was protruding oddly. Trent was injured. It was probably a broken collarbone by the look of it. Trent might want to take him down, but Daniel doubted he had the strength to do so. He might not even be able to shoot straight.

For a nanosecond, Daniel let his eyes dart to the open door to the adjoining motel room. He'd never imagined resisting arrest before. But these were hardly normal circumstances. Sarah might be safe inside Rita's trailer for now, but she was still his responsibility. Letting her sleep for a little bit was miles away from leaving her there in Rita's care indefinitely. No matter what happened next, he was pretty sure he could count on Chloe to look out for Olivia. But if he was arrested, handcuffed and taken off to prison, there'd be no one to safeguard Sarah.

"Daniel was only trying to protect me." Olivia stepped out from behind Daniel's cover. "He's a good man. He's probably the best man I've ever met. He's not a criminal."

An unexpected lump rose in his throat. He'd been called a lot of things in his life. Bodyguard. Giant. Guardian. Fool. But somehow no title had ever hit him as hard as hearing the certainty in Olivia's voice as she told the cop he was a good man.

Lord, she believes in me. Let me live up to the man I am in her eyes.

He looked from the cop with the gun in front of him to the woman standing by his side. Somebody had to step up, be the peacemaker and end this standoff.

"Trent, you're hurt. You need to see a doctor and I need to check in on Sarah." Daniel took a deep breath, set Chloe's gun down on the table in front of him and raised his hands. "But I'm not going to fight you. I just promise you, I'm not the kind of man you seem to think I am."

"Trent, listen to him." Chloe bent down and picked up her gun. "The Faceless Crew just blew up his place, too, and nearly killed the both of them."

"I can help you identify one of them," Daniel added. "I saw Shorty's face with his mask off." Daniel's eyes locked firmly and squarely on Trent's face. "I'm willing to cooperate and help your investigation any way I can. I'm not the enemy."

The cop hesitated. Daniel couldn't imagine the pain that would hit Trent's system when the adrenaline high he was running on wore off.

"Let Daniel go and I'll cooperate any way I can, too." Olivia pulled the photo memory card out of her pocket and set it on the coffee table. "I wanted to back these up before I turned them over to police, but here are all the pictures I took in the parking garage when Brian Leslie died."

"Put down the gun and let me check your injury." Chloe's hand swept Trent's left shoulder. "You know you're not going to arrest him. Any judge would toss the case out of court in a heartbeat. Besides, we're stuck here, and whether you want to admit it or not, you need his help. Unless you're really, truly convinced that Daniel is your guy."

Trent took a deep breath. His eyes rose upward and his lips moved in what looked like silent prayer. Then he dropped the gun to his side. "All right, I am not arresting you. But this is on the understanding that you've both agreed to fully cooperate with my investigation. Please don't make me regret this."

Daniel nodded. "Agreed. But you're going to have to let us know why the RCMP planted an undercover officer inside my ward's family company."

He'd gone without answers long enough.

"I'll tell you what I can." Trent shrugged, then winced in pain. "Can you just give us two minutes?"

"No problem." Daniel watched as Trent and Chloe walked into the adjoining room and closed the door behind them. Then he wrapped his arms around Olivia and held her for a long moment. Relief filled his chest like oxygen. "I'm glad you're okay."

"Yeah. Me, too." Her head rested in the curve of his chest, and it was all he could do not to brush his lips across her hair. He'd accused her of being so focused on her own priorities that she didn't care about anything else, and here she'd just gone and handed her photo card over to Trent when Daniel's freedom was on the line. "You going to go check on Sarah?"

"Soon," he said. "Very soon. I just want to give the cops a few more minutes. Hopefully, now we'll finally start getting some answers."

Even in hushed tones, just enough stray words managed to make their way through the paper-thin walls for Daniel to inadvertently piece together a pretty good guess of the conversation taking place on the other side. Somewhere higher up the police hierarchy, someone had decided Daniel was guilty of something involving organized crime and wasn't interested in hearing any of the other theories Trent had raised. Somehow knowing the cop had actually tried to argue Daniel's case actually made it a lot easier to cut him slack. Chloe, for her part, seemed plenty mad that Trent hadn't told her that her little sister was with Daniel at his house.

A gentle chuckle slipped through Olivia's lips.

He brushed his fingers along her cheek. "What's so funny?"

She turned her face toward him. "I wonder if Chloe's gun was really loaded. When you disarmed her, I mean. Knowing Chlo there's a small chance she *let* you take it from her, knowing the magazine was empty, just to prove what kind of man you really are. She's plenty tough, so it's hard to believe she'd allow herself to be unarmed like that. And there's no way she'll ever confirm it one way or another. But it's equally possible you caught her at an off moment and took her by surprise." Her fingers ran up the small of his back. "You do have some pretty impressive skills."

The adjoining door opened and the cops walked through. Daniel and Olivia jumped apart. Chloe's wig was gone now, showing tightly pinned hair, the same fiery red as Olivia's. Trent's right arm and shoulder were in an impressive-looking figure-eight sling. Hopefully that would help Trent keep the pain at bay and keep the injury from escalating, but he'd still need a doctor.

But I'm not his bodyguard, either, and can hardly force him to head to the hospital.

"How's your shoulder?" Daniel asked.

"Not great. Think my collarbone's busted. But I'll live. Okay, let's start again." Trent stretched his left hand toward Daniel. "Hello, I'm Constable Trent Henry, Royal Canadian Mounted Police. Please, just call me Trent. Not Constable and definitely not Henry. Olivia, we talked on the phone last night."

"Only your voice was a lot more chipper then," she said. "I'm guessing that was part of maintaining your cover?"

A wry smile turned at the corner of his lips. But he didn't deny it. "I'm part of a special task force investing organized crime in Canada."

"Like the Faceless Crew?" she asked.

"Like a lot of people." He leaned against the wall and got as close as he possibly could to crossing his arms. "My personal focus has been dealing with money laundering and tracking counterfeit currency. I've decided to take a risk here and tell you a whole lot of it passed through Leslie Construction."

Daniel would've laughed if the whole thing wasn't so deadly serious. "You're telling me that *Brian* was involved in laundering counterfeit money?"

"Yup." Trent nodded. "Brian had his fingers in all sorts of dirty money, and someone in organized crime was feeding it to him. I just wasn't in the company long enough to figure out who."

"So you cut Brian a deal on the back taxes and let him go in exchange for information?" This time the question came from Olivia.

"Well…" Trent ran his free hand through his hair. "Not me, personally. It wasn't my idea. But the tax people don't exactly go around asking everybody else's opinion when they decide to charge someone. They're a whole different animal. But yeah, Brian agreed to cooperate as much as he could. He had no idea who was really at the top of the pyramid. He was a drunk and a gambling addict. Someone was using him. Maybe several people. Brian was hardly the criminal mastermind type."

"But you figured I was." Now a laugh did escape Daniel's lungs.

Trent didn't even smile. "You mean, did I take a good, long look at the one guy who had a history with the Leslie family, happened to disappear overseas for ten years to travel around a virtual shopping list of locations known for their expansive underground criminal networks and then suddenly reappeared to take temporary hold of a big chunk of the family fortune? Seriously, Daniel? I wouldn't be much of a cop if I hadn't. Your background raised enough red flags to sail an armada—"

"I was escorting businesspeople and journalists through war zones! I was hardly hobnobbing with terrorists and drug smugglers."

"Which sounds all well and good in theory," Trent said. "But looked mighty suspicious on paper. I'm only trying to show you what things looked like from my bosses' perspective. Seriously, Daniel, what kind of man flies halfway around the world just to take guardianship of his cheating ex-wife's kid?"

"Mona was still my wife." Daniel crossed his arms. "My name was still listed in her will. Sarah's uncle was her only other family and I didn't trust Brian as far as I could punt him."

"Yeah, I get that." Trent nodded slowly. Daniel couldn't tell if the cop was resentful that circumstances had forced his hand or relieved to finally be having an honest conversation with him. "Anyway, that's where we're at. Any other questions? I probably can't answer them, but you can always try asking."

"What's my sister doing here?" Olivia asked.

"Like I said, I'm not here officially." Chloe glanced at Trent as though she was waiting for his permission to continue. He attempted another shrug. "It's more like professional courtesy. I looked into the case because of your phone call. That led me to talking to Trent. When he found out you were my sister, he asked if we could meet up. I opted to disguise my appearance, so as not to raise suspicion with other members of the crew. Hair like ours—" she nodded at Olivia "—tends to be pretty memorable, and I couldn't be certain I hadn't tangled with someone on the crew before. Someone who could recognize me. I was hoping to then head to Toronto and surprise you. But then the storm hit and we were trapped here."

"What do you mean trapped?"

Daniel directed the question at Chloe. But it was Trent who answered.

"Trapped as in trapped." Trent sighed. "As in we're stuck here, unable to go anywhere else. Believe me,

I wouldn't be standing around talking about this inside this dingy motel if there was somewhere else we could be." He pushed off the wall. "Thunderstorms were so bad most of Southern Ontario is now under a severe storm warning. Highway's flooded. Trees are down all over the place, taking down roofs and power lines. Roads in and out of the city are closed. Accidents everywhere. Last I heard, before we lost the cell signal completely, there were people sitting on the roofs of trains and cars waiting for rescue. Emergency services are struggling to respond. Only reason we're not flooded out here is that we're on higher ground, and the only reason we've still got some power is this place has a backup generator."

Daniel's spine jolted straight as the reality of the situation suddenly hit his overtired brain. "So Sarah probably didn't manage to call the cops on Rita's cell phone. Even if she did, no cops are on the way."

"Yup." Trent walked over to the window and looked out at the rain. "For right now, this lousy little motel is basically cut off from the rest of the world. If the Faceless Crew hit a flooded roadway or some kind of roadblock after torching your place, they might have very well ended up here, too."

FOURTEEN

Olivia's hand rose to her lips as the sense of safety she'd felt just moments ago while tucked inside the security of Daniel's arms was replaced with the sudden reality of just how much danger they were still in.

They were trapped. They couldn't leave. They couldn't get help.

So that was why Chloe had resorted to drastic, if misguided, actions to get her away from Daniel when she'd thought he was a threat. It was no wonder her sister had lost it when Trent had threatened to arrest Daniel. With no way to take Daniel to the station, he was basically looking at handcuffing him and leaving him in a motel room for who knows how long. "You think the Faceless Crew might be here?"

"It's just a guess," Trent said. "But a well-grounded one, unless they have a hideout somewhere in rural Ontario. Depending on where they were headed, they might not have been able to get on the highway. This is the only motel in the area. People have been arriving steadily through the night. At last check, there were about forty people staying in the motel and another eighty or so staying in the campgrounds. We haven't tried going door-to-door yet to see if there are any other law enforcement officers here because I'm not in a hurry to blow my cover. For now, it's best to presume that the circle of trust starts and ends with the four of us."

Daniel ran his hand over the back of his neck. "How long until they expect the roads to reopen?"

"Road north, maybe by sunup," Trent said. "Highway to Toronto could be shut until early afternoon. Last I heard anyway. Electricity and phone could take days in some areas. So I'm sorry, but it could be at least a day or two until we get a forensics crew out to whatever remains of your house. Now, if that covers everything you want to know, then, as you can imagine, I have quite a few questions for you."

"And I'm happy to answer them the best I can," Daniel said, "but first I've got to go get Sarah. I'll wake her up and bring her back here. We can continue this then."

"Understood," Trent said. "I'll come with you. I'll need you to let me know if you recognize anyone from the Faceless Crew. Hopefully you'll spot the one guy whose face you saw, but at the very least you can tell me if someone's build looks familiar. Besides, you'll have a much easier time finding Rita and getting her to let you talk to Sarah if I'm with you." Trent scooped the photo memory card up off the table and gestured to Chloe. "I'll get my laptop set up and maybe you can upload these photos while I'm gone so we can see what we're looking at there. I'll take a walkie-talkie so we can stay in touch. Also, someone should probably check in with the front desk about getting us new rooms where someone hasn't kicked in one of the doors."

Chloe nodded and followed Trent into the other room.

Olivia looked up at Daniel. "I'm coming with you, too."

"No, you're not," he said. "There's still a heavy storm out there, and the Faceless Crew have already made at least two attempts on your life."

"Just like they've tried to kill you." She stepped toward him until her toes brushed against his. "I can handle myself."

"I know." His hands brushed down her shoulders and onto her arms. "You're a live wire, Olivia. Which is awesome in a whole lot of ways. But not at a time like this. I want you to stay here with your sister, where you're safe. Lock the door and don't open it again until we get back."

He brushed a kiss over her forehead and started toward the other room. She just stood there a moment, watching him go. She could still feel the tingle of his lips on her skin. But this time his tenderness left her feeling anything but cared for. Didn't he realize he was talking to her like a child? She had so much respect for him. So why did it seem as if he had so little respect for her?

"No." Her voice seemed to echo in the wood-paneled room. He stopped in the doorway and looked back. "Look, I appreciate what you're trying to do, Daniel. But it isn't your call to make. You don't get to lock me up in a room and tell me to sit tight. I'm an adult. I'm a reporter. I'm not going to just sit by and let you sideline me."

"You're not a reporter anymore!" His hands shot up as though he didn't know whether to shake her or kiss her. "Don't you get that? Not right here. Not right now. Maybe you came up here yesterday as a reporter chasing a story. But now that story's gone. Sarah won't want to see you. I still have no idea why she's so hostile toward you. But the fact she was willing to trade you an interview in exchange for my friendship really worries me. It's immature and manipulative, and things between Sarah and I are complicated enough already with you being an additional complication. So I think the best thing for everyone is if Trent and I talk to Sarah without you there. I want to keep you and her as far away from each other as possible, at least until everything calms down and she's ready to make peace. If I don't see you before we leave, I'll try to touch base later. Okay? I'm just glad to know that for right now you're somewhere safe with someone who I know will take care of you."

He turned and started toward the other room without even waiting for an answer.

"You can't control everything, Daniel." The sound of her voice made him freeze in the doorway. But he didn't turn back. "You have such a huge heart. All you want to do is to protect everyone, and I know you're trying to manage everything the way you think is best. But it's as if you think if you just try hard enough you'll be able to hold your world together by sheer force of will. But Sarah's not Mona's little baby anymore. She's not even that teenager you saved from ending up in the foster system. She's months away from being a legal adult. She's going to be whoever she chooses to be, right or wrong, no matter how hard you try to protect her."

He didn't look back. She didn't step toward him. A long silence filled the space between them as she watched his shoulders rise and fall, and listened to the storm raging outside the windows.

"Well, I guess not everyone's as comfortable with chaos as you are," he said. "I won't leave her well-being up to chance just because she wants the freedom to ruin her life on her own terms. It's easy enough to stand outside the life of a person you've only known for a couple of hours and decide they're doing it wrong. But I can't talk about this now."

Daniel walked out and shut the door behind him.

She stared at the thin, scuffed plywood separating them, as if her eyes weren't yet ready to look away. Her heart felt numb, like the sensation of having adhesive ripped off your skin that nanosecond before the pain kicked in. Daniel was hardly the first person to decide she had no place in their life. Yet it was as if, as he'd walked out the door, he'd somehow accidentally knocked down the protective wall she'd built around her heart, leaving it aching for something she'd always craved and never known.

Her sister appeared in the doorway with a laptop in her hands.

"They're gone," Chloe said. "But the laptop can't read the photos on the memory card. He could barely get it into the slot."

"Probably because it was bent. I'll jiggle it." Olivia took the machine. Her voice sounded so tired it almost cracked. "Ricky, my photographer friend, showed me how. Reporters have damaged cards before and he'll just jiggle it around inside the slot until something makes contact."

She pressed the memory card as far into the slot as it would go, and then up. The card was in so deeply now it would probably take tweezers to get it back out again, and she wouldn't be surprised if she'd managed to damage the laptop slot.

The machine whirred. A window popped up on the screen. Five thousand photos started downloading. She sat down as a sigh of relief left her lungs. "I've got it. It's going to take a while, but we should have something by the time Trent returns."

"Just Trent?" Chloe asked.

"Daniel doesn't want to bring Sarah back here, because he thinks I'll set her off. And since protecting her is his priority, that means he'll stay with her. We didn't exactly say goodbye. But I wouldn't be surprised if I never saw him again."

"I'm sorry. I can tell you really like him." Chloe pulled a wool blanket out of a cupboard and dropped it over Olivia's shoulders. "Daniel likes you, too, you know. He likes you a lot, actually. I don't know what all has gone on between you two. But it's pretty clear he'd willingly risk his life to keep you safe."

"Because he's a former bodyguard. He'd risk his life for anyone." Olivia leaned back. "Don't get me wrong, he's a great guy. But you should have heard him trying to tell me to stay here and lock the door."

"He's overprotective because he cares about you," her sister said gently. "Look, I know this is a strange concept for people like you and me, considering how little attention Dad gave us. He was so focused on his own life he didn't think anything of letting us walk home from a new school, in a new town, all by ourselves. Remember that time we both got locked out in the snow because he ran off somewhere without checking whether or not we were inside? It taught us not to rely on any man. But not all men are like that. By the look of things, Daniel's pretty much the opposite of that." A smile crossed Chloe's lips. "I'm not saying that Daniel doesn't need to lighten up and loosen up, too. But maybe you could use someone like him in your life."

Someone like what? Reliable? Dependable? Steady? Rock solid?

Somebody she could count on not to let her down?

Olivia didn't know whether to laugh or cry. Sure, of course she wanted to find someone exactly like Daniel. But it seemed the last thing he wanted was to find someone like her.

"Maybe. But he's too far the other way, Chlo. He can't compromise. He can't take risks. I'm not even sure he knows how to listen. Being with a man like that would be like being wrapped in plastic bubbles and locked in an ivory tower. Even if Daniel was interested in keeping me around in his life—and I honestly don't think he is—I need more than just someone who wants me to be safe. I need someone who wants me to be me."

A group of Leslie Construction workers were drinking in a picnic pavilion and staring out at the rain. Young ones, mostly. Trent sauntered over, his stance loose and his posture arrogant. Daniel followed half a pace behind.

The guy might be a pain sometimes. But no one

could say Trent wasn't cut out for this kind of undercover work.

He was only sorry he'd missed out on hearing Constable Henry's "chipper" voice. Would've been fun to compare the two.

Connor and Jeremy sat on a table passing a bag of chips back and forth. Jesse was standing next to an open case of beer. Jesse's eyes flitted over Daniel's face for a moment, as if evaluating whether or not Daniel was about to start trouble over his stolen moment with Sarah. Then a grin spread across his face as though the young man was happy to see them. Daniel almost rolled his eyes. At least Sarah wasn't out drinking with them.

Jesse grabbed a beer out of the case and pitched it to Trent overhand.

Trent caught it with his left hand and threw it right back to Jesse. "Hey, any of you know where I can find Hawk and Rita? This guy's looking for Sarah."

There was a muttering of laughter. Then a couple of the guys pointed out into the woods.

"Hey, why don't you come hang out with us a bit!" Jeremy stumbled out toward them, his wobbly legs showing that he was way past sober. He jostled Trent as though they were two fans bodychecking each other at a sports event.

"Hey, man, watch it!" Trent yelped so loudly he almost swore. "I think my collarbone's busted or something."

"Whoa, sorry!" Jeremy raised his hands and only then seemed to notice the sling. "What you do to it?"

"It's nothing." Trent grinned. "Danny boy and I just had a bit of a dustup back at the motel. He didn't think the lady I was talking to was treating his lady right. You know how it is."

A laugh rolled off Trent's shoulders as if the whole thing was one big joke. A chuckle moved through the crowd as the guys laughed along with him.

"Who won?" Connor called.

"Go take a look at the motel railing. Then you tell me."

The men were still laughing as they walked off.

"Danny boy?" Daniel raised an eyebrow.

Trent chuckled for real this time and didn't answer. They pressed on through the rain until the pavilion party was out of sight.

Trent took a quick glance around, but there was no one there but trees and rain.

"Look," he said, "between taking down Hawk earlier and being willing to fight me, they're going to be looking at you a bit different now. The crew never had any respect for you, because basically they thought you were nothing but a pathetic idiot who Mona made a fool out of. Nothing personal, but it's not exactly easy for guys like that to get their heads around why you stepped up to become Sarah's guardian. I mean, everyone knew how wild Mona could be. They all know about her laundry list of short-term boyfriends—some of them were even on that list. In their minds, you've got every right to hate her. None of them can imagine doing anything to help the kid of a woman who'd treated them that way."

Daniel shrugged. "It was the right thing to do."

"Yeah, maybe. But they don't get it. How many of them think that way? Whole lot of them were willing to look the wrong way while Brian was cheating people, until they got cheated themselves."

"So the cops thought I'd become Sarah's guardian in order to launder money, and the Leslie Construction guys thought I'd done it because I was a wimp. Good to know."

"Hey, don't shoot the messenger!" Even in a sling, Trent managed to partially raise his hands. "The construction crew didn't think you were a bad guy. They just figured you were way too hung up on Mona to have eyes for anyone else. Looks as if they were wrong."

"What's that supposed to mean?"

Another chuckle. "Just stop beating yourself up for decking me back at the motel. Please. We both misunderstood what was going on, you weren't fighting dirty and it's not your fault the rail broke. Any decent guy who I'd respect would've done exactly what you did if they thought someone they cared about was in trouble. They just probably wouldn't have done it anywhere near as well. Besides, you helped me maintain cover, which is important because I'll need this identity intact even after the case is closed. I've been this guy on a couple different operations so far, as he's a handy cover to keep around."

They kept walking. The ground was slick with mud. Wind buffeted against their bodies. Lightning flashed in the sky above their heads. They started to jog. A tent blew past them, only to get stuck in a tree a few yards away. He could see glimpses of flattened, scattered campsites within the woods. Presumably their occupants had fled to the safety of the motel.

Unbidden, Olivia's face filled his mind. She was like a storm. Beautiful. Powerful. Wild. *If I was strong enough, I'd let myself love her. But she could turn me and my life inside out without even trying.*

They reached Rita's trailer. Trent banged on the door. "Hey! It's me. Anyone awake in there?"

Hawk opened the door. He took one glance at Daniel and swore.

"No way." Hawk slammed the door again. Trent rolled his eyes.

The door was pretty flimsy, Daniel noted. He could probably break in if he needed to. Just hoped he wouldn't have to. "Look," Daniel said, "I'm not here to cause trouble. I just want to see Sarah."

"She doesn't want to see you!" Hawk sounded drunk. There was the murmur of voices inside.

Daniel leaned against the trailer wall, feeling suddenly too tired to stand. It had been the longest night of his life. He'd never felt so defeated by circumstances.

You can't control everything, Daniel. Olivia's words flickered through the back of his mind. *You have such a huge heart... But Sarah's not Mona's little baby anymore... She's going to be whoever she chooses to be, right or wrong, no matter how hard you try to protect her.*

Daniel took a deep breath and prayed. *Lord, I'm tired. I'm sore. I'm soaked. All I can think about is the argument I just had with Olivia. I don't have the patience for Hawk right now. Please help me figure out what I can control and what I need to let go.*

"Hey, Rita?" he said. "It's Daniel. Look, I know you've never much liked me. To be honest, it's mutual. Definitely, I could've been nicer to you. I'm sorry about that. We both probably made things harder for Sarah sometimes than it needed to be." Silence fell within the trailer. No response. Hopefully she was listening. "Hopefully we can agree that we both want what's best for Sarah, even if we can't agree on what that is. I don't know if she told you, but someone broke into my house tonight and tried to kill us. I'm worried sick about her. I don't know if she's hurt. I don't know if she managed to call the police before the cell phones went out. Please, Rita. I'm not ordering. I'm asking."

There was a long pause. The door opened. Rita stood there. There was a scowl on her face, but at least the door was open. Hawk sat behind her at the small plastic table.

"Thank you." He stepped inside and out of the rain.

"Whatever." Rita rolled her eyes. She walked down to a closed door at the end of the camper. "You've got five minutes. But she's not going anywhere with you."

Trent followed them in. He dropped into a seat beside Hawk. "There's a bad storm brewing, you know. You'll all be safer in the motel. You don't want to get flooded out."

Rita rapped on the door. "Sarah? Baby? Daniel's here. Just wants to make sure you're all right." She glanced back at Daniel. "She's mad at us. She wanted to go partying with some of the younger guys. But we knew they'd be shooting up. Hawk and I told her we weren't letting her get mixed up with drugs under our watch, and that she had to stay put with us." She rolled her eyes. "We're not the total monsters you think we are."

"Thank you."

"Anyway, I don't know about the police. I didn't know someone had attacked your place. She didn't tell me what she was doing here and I don't ask questions. She did use my phone to try to call someone, though." She turned the handle and pushed the door open. "Sarah?"

Rita screamed.
The camper window was open.
The tiny bedroom was empty.
Sarah was gone.

FIFTEEN

Olivia lay on a vinyl couch in what passed as the living room area of a motel suite. The laptop was curled between her knees. After paying a sizable fee to cover the needed repairs to the door Daniel had damaged, they'd managed to move into a slightly larger, and far more expensive, pair of adjoining rooms farther down the floor.

The sound of the shower filtered in from the adjacent room. Chloe had gone to get changed into something more comfortable than the getup she'd worn as a disguise. Olivia had intended to try to sleep. Instead, she was clicking through photos.

The download was going a lot slower than they'd expected. Apparently the last couple of reporters to use the camera hadn't emptied it and the computer was downloading everything, starting with a few hundred photos of flower shows and arguing politicians.

Finally the photos from Brian's death had started to open. There were thousands of them. The camera had been set to keep clicking ten times a second once her finger had hit the button, and she'd gotten far more pictures than she'd expected.

Funny how the camera also seemed to pick up things she hadn't consciously noticed. First there was Brian coming through a door. He was looking around as if he was expecting to see someone. He'd been expecting company. Then he glanced behind him. *Hang on...* Was that a shadow or had there been a person behind him in the stairwell? Someone tall. Next picture, Brian was looking back again. His mouth was moving.

He was talking to someone.

She sat up and pulled the notebook out of her back pocket. The cover was damp, but the pages were dry. She flipped to a fresh one and started taking notes.

Brian Leslie hadn't been alone when he'd entered that garage. Someone else had come down the stairs with him. Someone who hadn't entered the parking garage. Also, Brian had clearly looked around as though he'd been expecting someone to meet them.

Photos kept downloading. She could see the Faceless Crew enter the frame now. Three figures, all in black, each with the featureless faces like a black fencing mask. A shiver shot through her body.

A doorknob rattled. A hooded face appeared at the window. Her hand rose to her mouth to stifle a scream.

"Olivia? Hey? You in there?" The voice was male, uncertain and familiar.

"Ricky?" She leaped to her feet and threw the door open. The young photographer tumbled in. She shut the door behind him. "What are you doing here?"

"I'm staying here." The photographer's earnest eyes opened wide. "After I talked to you on the phone, I called my mom and dad to let them know I was still on my way. Mom was all, 'No, no. It's going to rain a lot. You'd better not drive.' Even then I tried driving a bit, but the road was just a mess and no one was getting anywhere. So I made my way back here. Then I saw you heading up the stairs, and the hotel manager said he thought this was your room. What are you doing here?"

Her mouth opened and then shut again. It was not as if she didn't trust him. The story just felt so long she just didn't know where to start.

"Oh! You found a laptop!" Ricky dashed over to the computer and picked it up. "Whoa! Those are some seriously good pictures there. Wait until Vince gets a load of these! Looks as if you just saved both our jobs."

"Yeah, I guess so." Only that was a cop's laptop Ricky was now clicking through. But somehow it didn't feel right to blow Trent's cover without asking. "My sister's here, in the other room. That's not my machine. It belongs to the guy she was with."

He kept skimming through photos. "So is this guy going to email us a copy?"

"I'm sorry, Ricky. We might not get a copy of those pictures. Things got kind of complicated. We might not even be getting a story out of this."

"But this story was supposed to help us keep our jobs." His hands tightened on the laptop as if he was ready to clutch it to his chest and run. "I blew off a weekend assignment to come up here and help you land this interview. I lied to Vince because I thought you were going to pull it off. I trusted you."

"I'm sorry." She'd suspected he might have skipped a weekend assignment, but had no idea he'd outright lied to Vince. "I should have asked if you had another assignment. In fact, I should have trusted Vince and cleared this with him, instead of being impulsive and reckless and just rushing up here."

I should have stopped and thought things through. Now, because I didn't, I've potentially hurt Ricky. Maybe even cost him his job.

The door flew open. Daniel ran in. Followed by Trent. Suddenly everyone was talking at once.

"Daniel!" She jumped up. "Where's Sarah?"

"Who's that?" Trent asked. "And why is he touching my computer?"

"Hey, chill, dude." Ricky raised his hands. "I work for the newspaper, all right?"

Daniel's face was white. His knuckles clenched into two fists at his sides. Instinctively, she ran to him and slid one hand onto his arm. "Daniel, what's going on? Are you okay? Where is Sarah?"

"I don't know." He threw his hands in the air. "I don't have any idea anymore! Apparently Sarah had some kind of argument with Rita and Hawk and took off. She went to sulk in a back bedroom and sneaked out the window—they didn't even realize she was gone." He dropped down on the floor against the wall and sat with his head in his hands. "I give up. I don't know what to do. I can't protect her if she runs from me. She could be anywhere now. Out there, in a storm, with I-don't-know-who, doing I-don't-know-what."

Trent and Ricky were now arguing about the pictures. Something told her the future of her career might hang in the balance. But instead, she tuned them out and sat down on the floor beside Daniel. "It's okay. She's going to be okay."

"You can't know that." He looked up at her. "Even if she does turn up safe, just partying in some motel room with someone, next time she runs away I'll have even less ability to stop her. In a few months, my guardianship will be over, and I'll have no control over what she does. I've failed her. I tried so hard to be there for Sarah, just like I tried so hard to love Mona. But I let them down."

"No, you didn't." She slid her head onto his shoulder and felt the ruffle of his hair on her cheek. "It doesn't matter how good a carpenter you are. You'll never, ever build a wall safe enough to protect someone who doesn't want to be protected."

"Olivia?" Chloe's voice cut the air with a steady calm that sent shivers down her sister's spine. "We've got a situation."

And it was bad. Whatever it was, it was bad. That was Chloe's "there's a gunman behind you or a bear in the campsite" tone of voice.

"What's wrong?" She leaped to her feet. Trent stopped talking midword and shot Ricky a glare that implied if he didn't shut up quick there'd be trouble.

The room fell silent.

Chloe was standing in the doorway between the two rooms, dressed in a tracksuit with her long hair falling wet around her shoulders. Her face was the palest Olivia had ever seen it. Only the anger burning in her eyes gave away her composure. A walkie-talkie crackled in her hand.

Chloe held it out toward her sister. "Somebody wants to talk to you."

Olivia crossed the room, feeling her feet drag like lead with every step. Chloe squeezed her shoulder and put her lips close to her ear, and whispered so faintly she could barely make out the words. "It's going to be okay."

Chloe held the walkie-talkie up to her sister and pushed the button.

"Hello? It's Olivia. I'm here."

"Hey, sunshine. So nice to talk to you again."

Her knees shook. The voice was deep, gravelly and cruel. It was the voice of the man who'd stuck a gun in her face and forced her into a car. It was the voice that had threatened her on the phone at Daniel's. It was the voice she feared would always haunt her nightmares.

She pressed her lips together to keep back the panicked tears that filled her eyes.

Daniel crossed the floor in three strides. His arm slid around her waist. His hand cupped the small of her back, holding her firm. She closed her eyes and drank in the strength of her sister to her right and Daniel on her left.

Her voice was steady. "I said, I'm here. Who are you? What do you want?"

"You have something I want." The voice crackled. "I have something you want. I think we should meet and make a trade."

Daniel tightened his grip. Trent gave her a thumbs-up, then rolled his fingers in a "keep going" motion.

"What do you want?"

"You took certain photos I don't think you should have. You're going to give them back to me."

Her eyes slid to the laptop in Ricky's hands. *He wants the photos?*

"There's a little fairground on the very north corner of the property." The voice kept going. The raspy tone somehow sounded so terrifying despite being obviously faked. "Come through the woods. Stay off the roads. It should take you about half an hour to walk there, if you're good and quick. Meet me there in twenty-five. Don't be late."

She closed her eyes. "And why should I do that?"

The walkie-talkie crackled again. Then Sarah's panicked voice filled the room. "Olivia? Please. Do what he wants. Or else he's going to kill me."

SIXTEEN

Olivia felt her heart stop in her chest.

Daniel grabbed the walkie-talkie. "Sarah? Sarah? Where are you? Are you hurt? Hello? Hello?"

The walkie-talkie went dead. The room froze.

"They have her." He let go of Olivia and stumbled forward. His body shook as though he'd just been pulled from the rubble of an earthquake. "They have her and they're going to kill her."

Chloe left the channel open but muted the microphone so nothing they said would be overheard. White noise crackled. "No, they just threatened to kill her if we don't get them the pictures. That's all we really know for sure. Daniel, you know where this place is he was talking about?"

He nodded. "Absolutely. The motel owners tried to put in a little fairground a decade ago. It's a fully fenced-in area with a mixture of broken fairground rides and playground equipment. Some small buildings. Some signs. Lots of places for hostiles to hide. The parking lot has a separate entrance from the highway, but the fence around the actual fairgrounds has just one exit, so it'll be like walking into a pen. We can probably jog it through the trees in twenty. Any idea how they knew how to reach us?"

"My walkie-talkie is missing." Trent's voice was bitter. "I just realized after they radioed. It was on my belt when we headed out, and I don't know where I lost it. Maybe when one of the Leslie guys bodychecked me. Maybe when I was in Rita and Hawk's trailer. Or even in the woods. But somehow he has it now."

And Sarah.

"For all we know, someone's been spying on us." Daniel's eyes darted from the laptop to the window. "We've been careless."

His voice was so firm it was almost a rebuke. Olivia felt embarrassed, as if she'd let him down even though she'd closed the motel's flimsy curtains as best she could before loading up the machine and turned the screen away from the window.

Both the cell phone and landline phones were still down. Chloe set her watch to a twenty-five minute timer and set it on the table. She glanced at Trent. "Looks as though we're on our own. This is your case. What's the plan?"

Trent's skin was so ashen it was almost gray. Olivia couldn't imagine the level of pain he must be pushing through.

"Plan is we go get her." Trent adjusted the sling and sucked in a tight breath. "We go there and hand off the computer full of photos for the girl. Two cops against three killers isn't the best odds, especially with my injury, but I've survived worse."

"Four killers," Olivia said. "The man who just made the call isn't one of the Faceless Crew. I'm pretty sure he's whoever hired them. I think we even caught a shadow of him in the pictures."

Daniel's eyes fixed on her face. "Did you see a fourth person?"

"No. Just a shadow in the stairwell, and it looked as though Brian was talking to someone over his shoulder. But the voice on the walkie-talkie is the same as the guy who kidnapped me, and he doesn't match the body type of any of the three from the Crew."

Twenty-two minutes left on the timer now.

Trent glanced to Chloe. "I'll do the exchange. You provide backup. I'm shaky, so we'll need your finger on the trigger."

"It should be me." Daniel stepped forward. "With all due respect, you're too hurt to handle hand-to-hand combat if it comes to that, and I've done transactions in volatile environments before. Albeit not hostage negotiation, but some of the sticky situations I've been in came pretty close. I should be the one to walk into that pen. As far as we know, your cover hasn't been blown yet. Besides, I know the layout well. It was a favorite hiding place of Sarah's when she was younger. She'll understand what I mean if I give her cryptic directions."

The pain echoing in his eyes made Olivia's heart ache inside her chest. But command and control filled his stance and voice. She held her hands together behind her back to keep from reaching out toward him. She had to let him stay logical. It was probably all that was holding him together.

Trent and Chloe exchanged a look. Trent nodded and turned back to Daniel. "I hate to say it, but we're short on options and you're probably right about being the smartest choice. You go in. Chloe and I will keep you in our sights and provide backup. I have a spare bulletproof vest. Actually, I think between us we've got one for each civilian."

Ricky raised a hand. "Is it okay that I'm still really confused about what's going on?"

"I'm a cop. She's a cop. We're supposed to be undercover. His ward's been kidnapped. Someone will explain whatever else you need to know later. If you want to make yourself useful, take the photo card out of the computer."

"On it." Ricky nodded. "But I might end up wrecking it. It's pretty wedged."

"We'll have to risk it." Trent reached under the bed, pulled out a bulletproof vest and tossed it to Daniel. "We're giving them the laptop. It's clean except for the photos. I back up everything on an external drive. It'll be a better show of faith than just a tiny piece of plastic that's clearly damaged, and makes it look as though we're cooperating. We're just going to have to hope we'll be able to get the photos off the card again." He dumped three walkie-talkies on the bed beside Ricky. "You've got technical experience, right? Be useful and set these all to the same frequency."

"No problem." Ricky yanked the memory card free and stuffed it into his pocket. "I can set up a wireless video call between the laptop and our smartphones, too. Don't need internet, just wireless capability. That way the laptop will stream live video of whatever its camera sees directly to our phones."

Trent's eyebrows rose. "Yeah, do that."

Chloe checked her weapon. Daniel peeled off his shirt and slid on a bulletproof vest. Olivia sat. She

felt tiny and every bit as useless as that little powerless kid who used to stand in the kitchen too short to
even help pack boxes while her father's latest blowup
forced them all into another move. She wasn't six feet
tall. She wasn't trained in law enforcement. She didn't
know how to handle a weapon or set up a wireless
connection without the internet. Before this weekend,
she'd never stared down the barrel of a gun. She was
the only one here unable to help.

But the back of her mind was screaming there was
something important she was missing. That everyone
was missing. They were all being so logical, they were
missing the obvious—

"He asked for me!" The thought crossed her mind
so forcefully she nearly shouted it. "The guy who made
the ransom demand, he asked for me!"

"Honey, guys like that live off fear," Daniel said,
gently. "You're the weakest link and he knew he could
scare you."

She crossed her arms. "You can't possibly know
that. He just said *you*. He had no way of knowing who
I was with. What if he meant he wanted *me* to do the
exchange?"

"Absolutely not." Daniel pulled his shirt back over
the vest. "There's no way you're going in there."

"But I—"

His hand shot up. "Don't even start. Yes, I know
you're gutsy and plenty brave. But this isn't running
off to cover some random adventure. This is life-and-
death."

"You think I don't know that?" Her voice rose. "You
really think I *want* to just run into some creepy aban-

doned park knowing the Faceless Crew are lying in wait? Of course I don't. The thought terrifies me. But I heard his voice. He was talking to me. My instincts tell me that he wants me to hand over the photos. Not you or Trent or Chloe. Me."

Was that supposed to convince him? As if he wanted to think the same ruthless killers who had Sarah wanted Olivia in their grasp, too. "Your instincts are irrelevant right now."

"Instinct is nothing more than your brain suddenly catching up with what your subconscious already knows. Just because I don't think like you doesn't mean I'm wrong." She glanced at Trent. "We don't even know how he knows I had pictures from that night. Are you really going to risk sending the wrong person in there when someone's life is on the line?"

"I don't know what to think, and we don't have time to debate this." Trent looked from the clock to Chloe. "Thoughts?"

Chloe pressed her lips together. "If we go this route, Olivia's got this. I don't exactly like the idea of her being in danger. But if she's right and they want her to do the handoff I believe she can handle it. She's strong and has great instincts."

Daniel's eyes closed. *Lord, my heart is hurting so hard I can barely breathe. I hate everything about this. I'm already facing losing the ward I promised to protect. I can't handle losing Olivia, too.*

By the time he opened his eyes again, Olivia was already strapping on her sister's bulletproof vest. She pulled the sweatshirt over it.

"Can you guys give us a moment?" Daniel asked.

"Sorry." Trent scooped up the timer off the table.

They'd reached nineteen minutes. "You're going to have to talk while we run. I still think it makes the most sense if you're the one going in. You already have the training and I've seen you in action. Plus you're the girl's family. Whether you go in alone or with Olivia, you two can sort out. Now, everybody stick together. Follow my lead. Act casual." He tossed Ricky a laptop bag. "I can't make you come any more than I can force you to stay here. But as long as you keep out of the way and do what I tell you, I might be able to use your help."

They stepped out into the darkness. The rain had stopped, leaving nothing but a misty edge in the air. Trent led the way. His stride was fast but his posture still sauntered like someone not much caring where he was headed. Ricky followed with the laptop bag over his shoulder. Chloe came up the rear.

Which meant he and Olivia were right in the middle. Daniel slid his arm around her shoulders and pulled her closer. "I'm not okay with this," he said as they entered the path through the woods.

"I know." Olivia's hand brushed his back. "But it'll be okay. If I'm going to walk into danger, there's no one I'd rather have watching my back than Chloe and no one I'd rather have by my side than you—"

"No. I'm sorry. There's no way I'm going to risk walking in there with you."

His voice was louder than he'd meant it to be. Trent and Ricky glanced back. Olivia pulled away, bowed her head and kept walking. He'd hurt her, and knowing he'd done so ached like someone had reached in and hollowed out something inside his own chest.

Before he could explain, a hoard of Leslie crew came tramping through the woods toward them.

"Hey, dude!" Jeremy called. "Some trucker guy says the highway north and some of the back roads have re-opened. We're gonna try heading out."

"Catch you later." Trent gave them a wave and kept walking. "Try not to drown."

They hit an overgrown path. A gaudy face leered from the underbrush. The plaster clown pointed down the path toward the fairground. They started jogging, single file. The air was silent except for the sound of their feet hitting the wet earth and branches brushing past their bodies.

How do I possibly explain the way being this close to her throws my senses into chaos? I can't handle the way my heart aches at the thought of her being in danger. I can't handle the fact I'm falling for her. And even though she'll never be mine, I can't face the pain of losing her.

The path widened. There was a clearing ahead, then he saw the edge of the crude chain-link fence that surrounded the fairground. It was a great place to hide and a terrible place to get caught off guard. The gate was chained but still managed to hang open just enough for a person to squeeze through. Thick trees surrounded the complex on three sides. An empty road lay on the other. Inside the fence, there were a few small structures covered in graffiti, some rusted playground equipment and a smattering of coin-operated rides, including a four-seat Ferris wheel and small merry-go-round. Badly painted clowns peeked from every corner. There wasn't another person in sight.

There were four minutes left on the timer.

Trent handed out walkie-talkies. Daniel clipped his to the bulletproof vest and tucked it under his shirt.

"Everyone keep the channel clear," Trent said. "We want to be able to hear every word Daniel says and hear everything he hears. So, nobody gets on the line unless it's an emergency. Chloe, I want you to circle the perimeter. Our line of sight is going to be pretty terrible. Ricky, stay back and keep that phone link to the computer thing going and record the feed. Daniel, you'll go in the front gate in plain view. I'll stay in the shadows and provide backup. If I give the command to fall back, we meet back at the motel."

The cop glanced at Olivia. "Whatever you're going to do, you have less than sixty seconds to decide. Once that timer hits three minutes, I need everyone to be ready to go. As Daniel is the guy facing the guns, he makes the final call."

Trent pushed the timer into her hands. The others kept walking.

"Listen." Olivia grabbed Daniel's hand. "Please. I'm telling you, something doesn't feel right about this plan. Something's off. I can feel it in my bones."

"I know." Daniel squeezed her hand tightly. "But I have to do this alone. I can't have you walking in there with me. If you do, I'm going to be distracted. I'm going to be torn. It's going to make the situation so much more dangerous."

"You're wrong about me." Her voice broke. She dropped his hand and turned away. "You've got to know I'd never do anything to put Sarah in danger. I'm the one who ran to warn Sarah when the Faceless Crew showed up at your house. I know you don't believe in me and think I'm just some reckless, foolish liability—"

"No, I don't!" Gently, he ran his hands over her shoulders. He turned her toward him. "I think you're a beautiful, brave, strong, incredible woman who knows how to handle herself in a crisis. I think you're extraordinary. That's why I can't walk through that door with you by my side. You put *me* in danger."

He pulled her into his chest. His fingers ran down the small of her back. "Don't you get it? You rattle my brain, Olivia. You cloud my senses and keep me from seeing things clearly. I never should have let myself lose focus enough to escalate things with Trent. I never should have been sleeping in the garage loft, which allowed the Faceless Crew to sneak up on my house in the middle of the night without me knowing. I…"

He took a deep breath. She was so close now that all he'd have to do was lower his head and his lips would brush against hers. He gently pushed her back. "I never should have allowed myself to get emotionally compromised by getting close to you. I should have been smart. I should have kept my distance. Now all I can do is keep from making the same mistake again."

Please tell me you understand…

"Three minutes." She held up the timer. "Time's up."

They walked in silence down toward where Trent was standing by the tree line. Hot tears pressed against Olivia's eyelids with every step. But she refused to let them fall.

Daniel could have left it at no. Instead, he'd felt the need to tell her he regretted ever letting her close. How many times did Daniel need to show her that he didn't want her in his life? It was about time she believed him. And it was time she finally accepted a man like him had no place in her life, either.

All that mattered now was getting Sarah back safely.

"Chloe says the perimeter is clear," Trent said. "No people and no vehicles, as far as we can see. Inside the fence, though, is a different story. She's pretty sure she saw motion through the window of the smaller building. But we don't know how many people are inside."

"So it's probably a trap." There wasn't even a question in Daniel's voice.

"Likely." Trent nodded. "Either way, someone's going in. We can't take off and risk Sarah's life. Our top priority is getting the hostage out safely. You sure you still want to do this?"

"Absolutely." Daniel didn't even flinch. "I'm going in alone."

"Okay, then, Olivia, you're with Ricky. Your sister's scouted a location for you. Stay there. Stay silent. Stay hidden."

Something brushed Olivia's arm and she barely managed to stop herself from screaming. It was Ricky. He'd taken the laptop out of the bag and turned it on. The screen was open with the pictures showing. If she looked closely, she could see a video chat icon glowing in the corner.

"Guess this is when I hand over this," he said, "and you and I go hide."

"Yeah." But still her eyes lingered on Daniel. The thought of anything happening to him was almost unbearable. *Lord, please give him wisdom. Give him strength.*

His eyes met hers. Her voice broke. "Stay safe."

"You, too." Suddenly, Daniel was reaching for her. Strong arms pulled her tightly into his chest. Her hands slid up into the hair curling at the nape of his neck. He leaned his forehead against hers. She felt his breath on her face. "You stay out of the way and don't get hurt, okay? Promise me, regardless of what anyone else does, if I give you the signal, you'll grab Ricky and run back to that motel. You'll get yourself out of harm's way. Whatever it takes."

"But—"

His voice grew thick with emotion. "Promise me."

But... But... But...

Olivia, either you trust him or you don't.

She took a deep breath. "I will. I'll grab Ricky and run. What's the signal?"

He looped his finger around a strand of her hair and tugged gently. "Wildfire."

His lips hovered over hers. Her eyes closed.

The timer buzzed.

Daniel let go of her and took the laptop.

Ricky grabbed her arm and pulled her into the trees. "There's a flipped picnic table just around the corner. It's concrete. Chloe wants us to hide behind it."

Trent raised his weapon. Daniel stepped out of the trees and slipped through the gate.

"Hello? Hello?" Daniel walked slowly through the shambles of broken equipment, holding the laptop out in front of him. The soft light of the laptop screen lit the ground at his feet. "I'm here and I have what you want."

"Come on!" Ricky was practically running deeper into the woods now and yanking her after him. They reached the picnic table and slid down behind it. He pressed the walkie-talkie into her hand and held up his smartphone. They watched the screen. It was like some kind of small terrifying home movie. A broken swing set loomed in front of the screen's view, followed by some broken riding toys shaped like clowns.

"Daniel? Is that you?"

The camera spun and Sarah's face came into view.

"Thank You, God." Daniel's whispered prayer crackled softly through the walkie-talkie.

Olivia pushed herself up in a crouch to look over the top of the picnic table but couldn't see anything but fence and trees. Her heart ached to see his face.

I have to trust he'll be okay. I have to trust that Chloe and Trent have his back.

Then she glanced at the leafy darkness above her and felt her inner worries turn to prayer.

Lord, You know how hard it is for me to trust that anyone can keep their cool when things get tense. And You know that I'm always expecting every good thing I find to be snatched away. Please help me have faith. Please save them now.

Ricky tilted the screen toward her. She sat back down. Sarah was walking toward the laptop. Her hands were in the air. A mass of wires and what looked like a brick-shaped block of explosives were duct-taped to her chest.

She'd been rigged to explode.

Another camera shift and she saw tall, thin Rake, the so-called leader and brains of the Faceless Crew, holding a gun to Sarah's head. They were standing so deeply in the fairgrounds now there was no way the cops could get a clean shot through the fence.

"I have what you asked for." Daniel's voice echoed loud and clear. The camera shifted closer and higher, as if he was holding the computer up. "See, here are all the pictures. Every single one of them. We met our end of the bargain. Take them and let Sarah go."

Sarah's eyes darted past the camera. "Where's Olivia?"

"She's not here. Just me and the pictures. That's all they're getting." He took another step toward her. His voice dropped. "It's going to be okay. Are you all right?"

"Yeah." Sarah nodded. "I'm still alive anyway. But if they don't get what they want, this bomb is going to blow."

The camera swung to Rake. "You asked for the pictures. Here they are. Take them and let Sarah go."

Rake hesitated.

"But they don't just want the pictures." Sarah's voice rose so high she practically wailed. "They want Olivia."

"I know," Daniel said calmly. "I know she's what they want. But she's not up for negotiation."

He knew they wanted her? She'd thought he'd totally dismissed her hunch that the Faceless Crew wanted her, specifically, to make the exchange. But he hadn't been dismissing her. He'd been trying to protect her. Olivia could feel her heart shake inside her chest like an earthquake. Daniel took another step toward Rake. But Olivia turned her eyes away from the screen, lifted her gaze to the sky fading to light gray above her and focused her ears on the sound of Daniel's voice.

"It was Olivia who realized it first," Daniel said. "Her instincts are sharper than mine about some things. She realized your kidnappers wanted her here, trapped inside the fence in this pen. Now, I still don't know what whoever hired the Faceless Crew wants with Olivia. But I do know he wants to hurt her. I knew when I decided to take the risk of coming in here alone." He took another step forward. "No matter what you say and no matter what you do, know that *I won't let them hurt her.*"

"Is that what Olivia wants?" Sarah raised her voice until she practically screamed. "I know you're out there, Olivia! I know you can hear me! Do you want me and Daniel to die while you hide in the bushes? Once this bomb goes off, you're dead anyway. It's big enough to take out the whole area."

Olivia's limbs were shaking so hard she could barely move. She looked back at the screen. Rake raised his gun.

"Enough of this." Rake sounded angry. "I'm gonna count to five. Then I'm going to shoot Sarah in the head if that other chick doesn't come out here. And if she falls, she explodes. We all die. Got it?"

"Yeah," Daniel said. "I think I finally do get what's going on here."

Olivia closed her eyes and tried to pray. Ricky squeezed her hand.

"One…" Rake counted. "Two… Three… Four…"

"Wildfire!" Daniel slammed the laptop shut. The screen went blank.

Rake swore.

Sarah screamed.

A gun rang out.

But there was no explosion.

Olivia jumped up. Her hand clutched Ricky's. "Come on! We've got to run. Now!"

"But I didn't hear Trent give the order—"

As if either of them could hear anything now but shouting and chaos.

"Daniel gave it. Come on. For all we know this place might still explode."

For a moment she started toward the path. But Ricky yanked her back. "That'll take us right past them. We should take the road. It'll be faster."

He changed course and pelted toward the tree line.

"Hey, wait!" She ran after him. Daniel's words echoed through her mind. *Sometimes running is what keeps you alive. But sometimes running can get you killed.* Shouting and static crackled down the walkie-talkie. Sarah was screaming, but Olivia couldn't make out her words. The trees parted and they tumbled into a ditch beside the highway. A faint sliver of red brushed the horizon. A car was coming down the road.

"Hey! Hey!" Ricky started up the embankment. He waved his hands high over his head. The vehicle slowed. He glanced back, grinned. "It's the cops!"

The car screeched to a stop. Were the roads finally reopened? Had Sarah managed to call the police after all? A cop got out of the car. Large shoulders, terrible blond beard, mirrored sunglasses even though dawn had yet to break.

"I'm so glad to see you!" Ricky ran toward him. "There's a situation at the playground. We need your help—"

The uniformed man pulled out a gun and aimed at the young photographer. He fired. Ricky fell. Olivia opened her mouth to scream.

A hand clamped over her mouth.

Someone had sneaked up behind her.

The smell of something sweet filled her lungs.

The world began to swim out of focus.

Large hands lifted her into the air.

Desperately, she flailed at the man holding her.

The sunglasses fell off, showing a pair of cold gray eyes.

The fake beard came off in her hands.

"Told you I'd get my hands on you, sunshine."

Her body was tossed into the trunk of his car.

He locked her in.

SEVENTEEN

"One..." Rake was counting. "Two... Three..."

Daniel felt the world freeze around him. The bomb wasn't real.

He knew it deep in his gut with absolute certainty.

Maybe it was because Rake's posture was far too relaxed for someone standing next to an explosive he knew was live. The so-called head of the Faceless Crew had always made sure he was far away from the blast radius before. Maybe it was because the mass of tangled wires looked too much like someone's uninformed idea of what was supposed to be scary. Or maybe it was that even though Sarah's cheeks were wet with tears, her eyes had that same defiant, petulant stare she'd adopted when she was barely more than a toddler.

Instinct is nothing more than your brain suddenly catching up with what your subconscious already knows.

The Faceless Crew didn't want Sarah.

They wanted Olivia.

"Four..."

Daniel slammed the laptop shut and shouted for Olivia to run.

Rake froze. Daniel gripped the laptop with both hands and swung hard.

The blow caught the faceless thug on the side of the head. Rake stumbled back. His gun shot off into the air. Sarah screamed. In fear? No, rage. One swift punch to the jaw and Rake fell to the ground. The gun dropped from his hands. Daniel threw the laptop at Rake and leaped for the gun.

Then Daniel wheeled around, the gun safe in his grasp. "On your knees. Hands on your head." Rake knelt. "Now take off the mask."

The faceless thug pulled his mask off and tossed it into the dirt.

The sallow face belonged to a stranger.

Another stranger.

Where were the rest of the Faceless Crew? The back of his spine tingled. *Lord, what am I'm missing here?*

"Daniel, hand me the gun." Sarah reached out her hands. "I'll point it at him while you find something to tie him up."

"No. I'm sorry." He shook his head. The wire contraption had come loose from Sarah's chest during the struggle and was hanging sideways. No timer. No detonator. No explosives. Just wire, duct tape and an empty box. It was all just a sick and violent charade. He yanked it off and she grabbed for the gun. But his other hand held it back at arm's length. "I don't know what kind of game you think you're playing, Sarah. But it ends here and now."

A sound like a gun blast echoed from beyond the trees. Then the distorted sound of Ricky screaming took over the walkie-talkie hidden by his shoulder. "Hello? Hey, Ricky? Is Olivia okay?"

Too late he heard the click of a gun. He turned back.

Sarah clutched a small handgun. Her arms shook, but she kept the barrel pointed straight at him. "Sorry, Daniel. I won't let you ruin my life anymore. Now just keep quiet and let me walk out of here."

I promised to be her guardian. No matter what. Lord, help me keep my promise now.

"Trent!" he yelled. "This whole thing's a setup. Sarah's working with the Faceless Crew."

Sarah swore. "Trent's a cop?"

Rake took advantage of their distraction to leap up off the ground. He started for the fence.

Trent ran through the gate after him.

Daniel threw himself at Sarah. The gun went off in her hands.

The kickback sent the bullet flying over his head.

Daniel tackled her, bringing his ward to the ground.

She dropped the gun. He reached for it.

Sarah kicked him in the jaw, squirmed from his grasp and ran deeper into the broken fairground.

"I've got him." Trent was standing over Rake. With his one good hand he'd somehow managed to pin the thug in a headlock. "Doesn't look as though the rest of the crew are here. Chloe's gone to find Olivia and Ricky. Try to catch Sarah."

This time, she wouldn't be getting away.

Daniel turned and ran after her. She darted into the warped and broken remains of a mirror maze.

"Enough." He caught her by the arm and spun her back around. "No more lies. You were the one who lured Brian into the parking garage that night, weren't you? He told you he'd made a deal with the authorities."

The rising sun was brushing the horizon now, rays

of light hitting the fractured reflections around them. Sarah wouldn't meet his eyes. "You don't know anything," she argued mulishly.

She tried to pull away. But his grip held her fast.

"No, I know plenty. I just never put the pieces together until I saw you stand there and demand Olivia come out and turn herself over to killers to save your own selfish neck. Brian was never smart enough to pull this off on his own. But you, Sarah. You had all of your mother's street smarts and your grandfather's business savvy. Brian probably didn't know half the things you'd gotten the company into. I'm right, aren't I?"

"So what?" Sarah shouted. Her fists beat against his chest. "What are you going to do about it? Everyone knows you won't let me go to jail. You think Mom stayed married to you because she cared about you? She wanted you to be my guardian because you're nice. Because you're a pushover. She told me, when she knew she was sick. She promised me that if I agreed to live with you, as my guardian, just until I could inherit my money, you'd protect me from Brian without messing up my life."

Yeah, Mona had never understood his wedding-day promise to love her unconditionally. So she never would have understood what lengths he'd go to love and protect her daughter, too.

The fierce, anxious need to protect her that he'd felt ever since he'd first laid eyes on the tiny baby in Mona's arms broke like a cresting wave and flowed like sadness over his chest. Her shouts rose until they were nothing but a wail of fury. Her hands beat against him, harder and faster, until so much anger surged through her frail form that she tried to claw at his face. Gently but firmly, he pushed her back against the mirrored wall. Then he turned to the walkie-talkie. "I've got her, but I need a cop to take over now."

Her face paled. "You're not going to tell on me or let them arrest me. You promised to look out for me."

"I'm going to keep that promise by seeing you face justice."

Her jaw dropped. "This is Olivia's fault, isn't it? He told me not to trust her. When I wasn't sure I could go through with helping him kill her, he showed me a picture he took of the two of you all cozy inside the diner, holding hands. Told me if she didn't die, she'd sway your heart, poison your mind against me and ruin everything."

"Who, Sarah? Who's *him*? What does he have against Olivia?"

"He's the man who's going to catch her and kill her. And I won't tell the police anything to help stop him unless you agree to meet all my demands. You're going to help me, you're going to make sure I don't go to jail and you're going to promise me you'll never speak to Olivia ever again."

"I'm not going to be blackmailed, Sarah. You're not calling the shots. Not anymore."

Sarah spat in his face. Daniel just wiped his cheek with his shoulder without loosening his grip.

"Daniel!" Chloe appeared around the corner, gun in one hand, badge in the other. "We've got a situation. Ricky's been shot and Olivia's gone."

EIGHTEEN

Daniel felt all the blood drain from his face. "What do you mean Olivia's gone?"

"She was abducted by someone in a cop car." Chloe's face was grave. "A fake one, judging by what Ricky said about the markings."

"So he got her anyway!" Sarah said. "Good. I'm glad."

"Who?" Daniel's limbs fought the urge to shake answers out of her. "Who's after Olivia?"

"My boyfriend." She grinned. "My hot, powerful, secret, well-connected boyfriend who my stupid guardian didn't know I had."

The world spun around him. He closed his eyes. He'd tried so hard to steer her in the right direction and her path had ended up even more crooked than he'd feared.

Lord, how did this all go so wrong?

Anger battled inside him, and for a moment he was afraid it would take him over. Then he remembered the fierce determination he'd seen so often burning in Olivia's eyes. She didn't fear her emotions. She harnessed them and turned them into strengths. He took a deep breath and focused on the feeling of the solid ground beneath his feet.

"Who is he?"

"I'm not telling you that!"

He opened his eyes and let her see the depths of emotion burning inside them. "Sarah? Your so-called boyfriend is nothing but a violent criminal who's mixed up in organized crime and used a vulnerable teenage girl to launder money through her family business. He's not here for you now—he left you to get caught and turned over to the police. That tells me he doesn't care about you at all."

"He loves me!" She was trying to sound so tough, but all he heard in her voice was the wail of the same self-destructive girl he'd spent the past four years trying to keep out of jail. "And he'll come back for me once Olivia is out of the way. He has big plans and really dangerous friends. He was only at Leslie to sell drugs for his boss. But he figured out how we could work together to use the company to launder money. When I get control of my inheritance, he's going to help me run the company. We're finally going to be together and I'll never have to go back to your horrible country house. He says the only person who can link him to Brian's murder is Olivia. He's going to kill her and bury her body and then burn everything down around her so you'll never, ever find her."

Chloe tapped Daniel gently on the shoulder. He stepped back and released Sarah. Chloe snapped a pair of handcuffs on her. He followed them out. Sunlight brushed the top of the trees, showing him the tears that glinted in the depths of Chloe's green eyes. Eyes that looked just like Olivia's.

Ricky was sitting on the ground leaning against the

fence. "Hey, I'm sorry. I let him take her. I should've been able to stop him."

"It's not your fault." Daniel crouched beside him.

Trent walked over, pushing Rake in front of him. The thug's hands were cuffed behind his back and his eyes were focused on the ground. The other two members of his Faceless Crew were out there somewhere, and something told Daniel getting Rake to talk wouldn't be easy.

"Vest stopped the bullet from killing Ricky," Trent said, "but he's probably looking at a couple of broken ribs. Northbound highway's open. Chloe's going to drive Ricky to the hospital. I'm going to drop this joker off at a station. Can you drive Ricky's car? Then we'll all meet at the hospital, loop in our colleagues and strategize a plan for finding Olivia. Don't worry. We'll bring her back alive."

Daniel walked back to the motel like someone sleepwalking through fog. His brain told him he'd been awake for almost twenty-four hours. His heart ached as though he'd never sleep again.

He drove, barely aware of what he was doing. The highway had been reopened for over an hour, and now an endless stretch of bumper-to-bumper traffic was inching forward slowly. Chloe and Trent had flown up the shoulder with emergency vehicle lights on the tops of their cars.

But Daniel could barely do more than ease his foot on and off the brake.

Lord, I can't remember ever feeling so powerless. I need Olivia to be safe. I need her to be okay.

A morning sunrise filled the sky in a fresh wash of blue. He could barely take it in. His heart felt like someone had burned it out from the inside leaving nothing but ashes. Split trees and downed power lines dotted the forest on either side. Even if his house had survived the blaze from the garage explosion, there could still be a storm-toppled tree or two through his roof.

I'll never have to go back to your horrible country house... He's going to kill her and bury her body and then burn everything down around her...

Sarah's foolish bragging flashed like lightning through his mind.

Then he remembered Olivia's words after the Faceless Crew had blown up the garage. *He said the client might even make them go back and torch your house...*

His house.

The Faceless Crew had taken Olivia to his house.

He pulled out of traffic and did a U-turn into the lane heading south. His foot pressed the accelerator. He was heading home. He had no proof that was where she was, no weapons and no way to call for backup. Just the strong, sudden impulse to act, burning through his veins like wildfire. Every synapse of the man he'd always been told him it made far more sense to inch his way to the police station and let the cops form a sensible, practical search plan.

But that could take hours. Olivia didn't have that long.

And he knew without a doubt that she'd have done the same for him.

He flew past the motel and turned onto the road that would lead him home. It was inches deep in water. The spray rose up like curtains on either side of Ricky's car. He passed the small ghost town where he and Olivia had stopped to escape the storm, then continued until he was less than a ten-minute walk from his home. A ramshackle barn appeared ahead on the side of the road. He parked behind it and popped the trunk to see if there was anything in there that might double as a weapon.

Ricky had a toolbox. A small knife went into one front pocket. A screwdriver went into another. He slung two bungee cords around a wrench and a roll of duct tape. He attached them all to his belt. Then he slipped into the trees and started running.

Lord, I've never felt so unprepared and unequipped. I don't even have the cover of darkness to hide me. Help me get Olivia out safe. I really don't want to imagine life without her.

The familiar walls of his house loomed ahead through the trees. It was still standing. His footsteps slowed. There was no sign of movement. Not a single vehicle parked in the driveway. An ugly pile of twisted metal and ash lay where his barn garage and truck had been.

Had he guessed wrong? Was Olivia not here after all?

No, wait. A short faceless figure dressed all in black was pacing the lawn, a gun in his hand. Shorty was guarding the front door. Daniel crept around the side of the house and saw a flash of red in the side window. He raised his head just enough to look in.

Olivia was standing in the pit of his living room foundations. Her head was bowed toward the ground. A man in a fake police uniform with messy blond hair pointed a gun at her. The sight of her was enough to make hope leap in Daniel's chest. Olivia was trapped. She was in danger. He didn't know how to reach her, help her, to even let her know he was there.

But thank You, God. Olivia is alive!

The man moved to the side and Daniel felt the flicker of joy die in his chest.

There was a shovel in Olivia's hands.

Her captor turned.

It was Jesse.

He was making Olivia dig her own grave.

The shovel shook in her hands. The gun pressed into the back of her head.

"Keep digging."

She gritted her teeth. Her stomach was still upset from whatever had been on that cloth he'd clamped over her face. But it couldn't match the turmoil in her mind.

Jesse.

How had she not recognized him before? The angry fake cop with the bushy fake beard who'd tried to stop her from following Brian to the parking garage was the same gravelly voiced man who'd threatened her over the phone, tried to kidnap her outside the diner and demanded the photos over walkie-talkie—and the same fake, charming man she'd fought when she'd caught him alone with Sarah.

The only thing he'd never been able to hide was the hatred in his cold gray eyes. Now they were alone, and the mask was finally gone as he ordered her to dig a hole in the foundation of Daniel's living room for him to bury her in.

The hole at her feet was at least three feet long and almost two feet deep now. She kept digging. Slowly. Buying time. The moment she'd been lifted out of the trunk and felt her feet touch ground, her first impulse had been to run.

I would have done it if not for Daniel's words shooting through my brain. "Sometimes running is what keeps you alive. But sometimes running can get you killed."

She hadn't taken his words to heart when she'd first heard them. In fact, not long after he'd said them she'd run toward a kidnapper's car thinking it was Ricky's and then pelted into the abandoned strip mall to escape Jesse, without even realizing the headlights ahead of her were Daniel's. Those same words had flashed again through her mind when Ricky had run toward the road and into danger.

So when Jesse dragged me out of the trunk and dropped my feet on the ground, I paused. Long enough to think. Long enough to realize her wobbly legs would've dropped her to the ground before she could get very far. Just long enough to spot Shorty and Brute in the shadows and to notice when Jesse sent Brute to watch the road and left Shorty on the front porch. Long enough to remind herself that if Jesse thought she was cooperating, it would buy time for a rescue. Which might be the only reason she was still in one piece and digging this hole.

"So you decided you needed to kill me when Sarah told you Daniel wanted her to meet a reporter who'd survived the parking garage bombing? You realized I might be able to identify you as the cop I'd argued with just before Brian was killed, right? I might even have a picture of you following him to his death on my camera. Must have scared you to realize someone could link you to Brian's murder. Is that why you used

Brian's computer to invite everyone up here for a fake party? To pressure Sarah into helping you kill me?" No answer. She dug a few more shovels full. "No wonder she looked terrified when I walked in on you two in the bedroom. Probably worried what two murders would do to her image."

"Shut up about Sarah." The sound of gritted teeth in his voice told her more than any words could about just how accurate she had been. "Keep digging or I'll cuff you upside the head."

He'd cuffed her a few times already. So many times in fact, that she was now able to sense it coming. The gun would leave her skull. His arm would pull back. Then a sudden blow would snap her head forward, filling her vision with stars.

There was a sound of a voice outside. A muffled syllable. Nothing more. A dull thud of something hitting the ground. Then the slightest tapping sound, like fingers drumming on the windowpane. She pressed her lips together and counted. One long. Three short. Three long.

"Rumor has it that all this links back to organized crime." Olivia dug her shovel deep into the soil, fighting to keep her body language neutral, not to give anything away. Her hands tightened their grip on the handle. "But let me guess. You're a very minor player in a big operation, which is why you had to hire an incompetent gang of thugs to do your dirty work. Oh, your bosses are into big things—counterfeit bills, money laundering, drug trafficking, illegal gambling. But you, you're a nobody. A loser who got embedded in some minor construction company because he wasn't even making enough money on crime to get by. But you met a pretty and vulnerable teenage girl with a big inheritance coming to her and realized you could use her, her money and her company to really get somewhere. Get her to fall in love with you, and you'd finally be able to make a big name for yourself in organized crime, laundering money and who knows what else through her company. Must have driven you mad when the tiny little woman you were trying to kill managed to pull you off her and get the better of you."

"I said, shut up!" The gun pulled away from her head just long enough for him to bring his arm back to swing again.

This time, she wasn't about to give him a chance to let him land the blow.

Olivia swung around, ducked under his fist and threw a shovel of dirt in his face. He swore and grabbed his eyes. She brought the shovel down hard on the side of his head. The gun flew from his hands and disappeared into the foundations. Jesse landed on his knees and rolled onto his back, groaning in pain.

Olivia scrambled across the dirt floor.

A tall, broad-shouldered figure stepped into the doorway, backlit by the morning sun.

A cry left her lips. "Daniel!"

"Hello, you." His hand reached down and grabbed hers. In one swift motion, he pulled her up out of the pit and into the strength of his arms. The smile that filled his eyes set lights dancing inside her heart. "You have no idea how happy and relieved I am to see you."

"Me, too." Despite the pain and fear she couldn't stop an exhausted smile from brushing her lips. "Where's Sarah?"

"Safe but under arrest." His face darkened. "She was working with Jesse."

"I'm so sorry."

He sighed. "Me, too."

Jesse was still down on the ground at the other end of the living room pit, swearing as he searched for his gun.

"Are there more of them?" Daniel asked.

She nodded. "Brute is patrolling the woods. If we're not careful, we'll run right into him."

"Too bad. I'd have loved to have the time to go deal with Jesse properly. But I don't want to risk Brute coming back shooting while I'm busy knocking Jesse out." Daniel pulled her out onto the porch and slammed the front door, then used a bungee cord to attach the handle to the railing. "Locking him in will have to do for now. Won't last long. But it should buy us a small head start."

She glanced around the lawn. Shorty was lying on the driveway. His eyes were closed but his chest was still moving. "Once I heard him fall and you tap my initials, I knew it was time to get ready to run."

"You managed to catch all that?"

"Of course. The hardest part was trying to think like you, pay attention and fight the urge to just run off wildly."

"Well, we both seem to have learned something from each other." Daniel's hand tightened in hers. "Come on, we've got to run. I did manage to grab Shorty's gun, but I'm hardly going to launch into a gun battle with illegal weapons against a killer if I can help it."

A gunshot blast sounded from the living room behind them. The door frame exploded into splinters. Looked as though Jesse had managed to find his gun.

Then a second bullet flew past from the other direction. Brute was running down the driveway toward them. He was still probably too far away to get in a fatal shot. But he was closing in fast. One gunman behind them. One in front of them and getting closer.

They were trapped in the middle with nowhere to run.

Olivia wheeled around to Daniel. "Now what?"

"Up." Daniel jumped on the porch railing. "We've got to climb."

NINETEEN

"Come on." Daniel pulled her up onto the railing. "We're going to climb onto the porch roof and up onto the second floor."

"What?" How was that not a death trap? "We'll be cornered up there with two men shooting at us."

"Please." He reached up and grabbed the shallow roof above their heads. His eyes grew darker as they fixed on her face. "I have my firearm stashed up there. I took out their explosives guy and destroyed the only bomb Shorty had on him, which he never even got a chance to set. Considering how wet the wood is, unless they brought a foolproof backup bomb, or they've got a major accelerant handy, I can get up there, arm myself and come back faster than they can set this place on fire. Trust me. It's the best option we've got."

I want to trust you. But this is crazy! "You said the second and third floor were in such bad shape we were likely to fall through."

"I know." He let go of her hand and hauled himself up onto the roof above her head. "But I also went through and painstakingly marked on the floor where all the main supporting walls were. If we stick to my path, we won't fall through."

She scrambled up onto the railing and reached up with both hands. He grabbed her by the wrists and pulled her up onto the porch roof. It shook under their weight.

Jesse broke through the door beneath them. Brute shot toward the house again, but only managed to elicit a burst of swearwords from Jesse.

"This way!" Daniel yanked a window open. They tumbled into a huge master bedroom. The crescent-shaped room had huge windows and several boards missing from the floor. Fluorescent spray paint traced a single vertical line across the room. So not a lot of supporting walls under this room, then.

She leaped to her feet only to feel her right foot punch a hole through the worn floorboards all the way to her knee. Daniel grabbed her hand and helped her out. "Careful. Probably best we stay on our hands and knees until we're out in the hallway."

They crawled along the thick fluorescent line and through the doorway. A bullet flew up through the floor where her foot had been. They reached the hallway and started running single file. Her eyes barely took in the rooms on either side, drinking in the beautiful, ragged empty spaces with no doors, holes in floors and huge broken windows.

There was shouting beneath their feet, followed by a blast of gunfire and the sound of floorboards splintering behind them. They hit the end of the hallway. A door flew open in front of them. Brute was standing there at the top of the stairs with a gun in his hand. He leveled them in his sights.

"Get down!" Daniel yelled. He raised his hand above his head and spun something around like a slingshot. She dropped to the floor just in time to see it fly through the air. The projectile caught the huge thug in the chest. Brute grunted, fell back, then suddenly dropped from view like a stone.

A deafening crash filled the air.

They reached the doorway and looked down through a gaping hole at the pile of broken timber that had moments ago been the rickety staircase. She grabbed the wall to steady herself. Brute had fallen straight through.

"Told you those stairs were dangerously unsafe." Daniel's hand touched hers. "I just pray he manages to stay alive until we can get out of there and send an ambulance for him. He might be a killer, but I'm not."

"What did you throw at him?"

"A wrench attached to a bungee cord. I just wanted to knock him out, and I guess I shouldn't be surprised his fall took down the stairs."

A bullet shattered the door frame beside them. Daniel yanked her back against the wall. A second hole appeared in the ground by their feet. All three of the Faceless Crew were now accounted for. But Jesse was still shooting. She didn't want to know how many holes it would take through the floor before the whole thing collapsed beneath them.

"This way." Daniel pulled her through a doorway and into a narrow staircase. "We need to keep climbing."

They couldn't head down. They couldn't stay where they were. But would climbing up higher make them any safer? Daniel was already heading up the narrow, darkened staircase. "Hug the wall and watch your step. Some of the stairs are missing."

She climbed up behind him. They came out into a small, dusty attic. The ceiling slanted steeply above their heads. A large window looked out at one end of the room. Rays of sunshine spread out across the dingy floor.

Daniel looked around the empty space and groaned.

"What?"

"I kept my hunting shotgun up here. It was in a locked box under a tarp. It was the most obscure, unlikely place I could think to hide it, because I didn't want Sarah stumbling upon it. She could be pretty nosey but she knew she wasn't allowed up here. Figured she'd be afraid of crossing the floor. Guess I was wrong." He sighed. "I do have the gun I lifted from Shorty. It's a horrible piece, totally illegal and only has two bullets left. But it's better than nothing. At least we managed to take out the Faceless Crew, so it's now just Jesse we have to worry about. Sarah made it sound as if they were planning on blowing the house up, and when I took out Shorty he had an explosive device on him. Looked as though he hadn't set it yet. I managed to slice up the wires pretty good, then yanked the whole contraption apart and tossed it in a puddle. Hopefully, Jesse doesn't have the technical know-how to put it back together."

Daniel crossed over carefully to the window at the front of the house and looked out. She did, too, but saw nothing but an empty driveway fading into the tree line. More bullets sounded below them. Then came the sound of Jesse bellowing and shouting words she couldn't make out. Daniel sat on the floor against the wall and gestured for her to join him. She sat beside him. Her head dropped against his shoulder. "I'm really sorry about Sarah."

"Me, too." He slid one arm around her shoulder and pulled her close to him. "Ever since I became her guardian, I had this feeling I was just treading water trying to keep her out of jail. I think I had mostly forgiven myself for everything that had happened with Mona, but I hadn't quite been ready to get rid of this nagging feeling that if I'd only loved her just a little bit harder, she'd have given up the drugs and the partying, and her life would've turned out differently. I think I needed to spend the past few years working this hard at taking care of Sarah for God to show me that no matter how hard you try to guide someone's life, people are still going to make their own choices. You helped me see that, too." His arm tightened around her. "I'm just thankful Sarah's still alive and safe in police custody. Maybe she'll get the kind of help she needs behind bars."

"Now what?" She couldn't remember ever feeling so trapped and helpless. There was nowhere left to run. Nowhere to go. Yet somehow with Daniel beside her, sitting in the attic of this ramshackle old house, she felt the most at home she'd ever been.

"First we pray and thank God we're here, still alive, still together. Then we make a plan for getting out of here alive."

She closed her eyes for a moment and lifted her heart toward God as Daniel whispered a prayer into the darkness. They squeezed each other's hands tighter than she'd ever held on to anything in her life.

Lord, I'm not ready to die. Not here. Not now. But

thank You that I met a man like Daniel. Thank You for showing me there are people I can rely on when the world all falls apart. Thank You that he and I are in this together.

Then she felt Daniel's lips brush against her hair. "We'll figure something out. I drove Ricky's car here and it's parked not that far away, if we can get down safely and run to it."

The sound of gunfire stopped below them. She didn't know if that was a good or a bad sign. "Does anyone else know we're here?"

"No, I'm sorry. Trent took off to coordinate with the police and turn over Rake. Your sister took Ricky to the hospital. The bulletproof vest saved his life. We just have to pray they'll put two and two together and figure out where I went." His hand brushed up her neck and under her chin. She turned her face toward his. "I'm sorry. I wish I'd handled things differently. Maybe if I had, we wouldn't be here. I wish I hadn't tried to stop you from following your gut. I wish I hadn't told you to run—"

His voice caught in his throat. Her fingers ran up the back of his neck.

"And I wish I hadn't rushed up here Friday night with Ricky to interview you the way I did without clearing it with my editor," she said softly. "We both made a lot of decisions, some right, some wrong. But we're here now, and like you said, we'll find a way out of this."

"Yeah." His voice grew husky. "At least we're together now."

His face bent toward hers. Then she felt his lips brush over hers.

Something crashed outside.

"What was that?" Daniel jumped up and walked over to the window. She followed just as an angry shout filled the air.

"You want to stay up there? Fine, then you can die up there!" Jesse was standing on the lawn, staring up at them. In one hand he clutched a gun. In the other he held up a jug of gasoline. "You may have destroyed my bomb, but I'm going to set fire to the house. I promised I'd burn you down. One way or another, you're going to burn!"

She watched in horror as Jesse dragged the can up onto the porch. The smell of gasoline wafted up toward them. He sloshed gas wildly over the wood. The stone walls themselves wouldn't catch fire. But the blaze would still burn the floorboards out from under their feet—if the smoke didn't choke them first. Even if they climbed to the roof, Jesse could watch and shoot while the house raged into an inferno beneath them.

They'd run out of time. They'd run out of options.

In moments the porch would be ablaze.

Daniel slid the windowpane all the way up.

"Come with me." He grabbed her hand and pulled her back through the attic, away from the window. "I have a plan—"

"Plan? What plan?"

"No time to explain." He turned them back toward the window. "Just get ready to jump."

"What?"

Jump? What kind of plan is—

"Go!"

She felt the pull of his hand on hers and held on to him tight.

They ran, pelting across the attic floor.

The window grew closer.

"Lord, You are our ever-present help in danger… Now!"

Daniel leaped through the window. Olivia followed one footstep later.

They plunged through the air. Then hit the top of the porch. The sagging wood smacked hard against her body. The breath was knocked from her lungs. She lost hold of Daniel's hand.

The roof gave way and they fell through. Wood splintered around them.

Jesse glanced up in horror as Daniel, Olivia and the entire porch roof fell in on top of him.

Lord! Save us! Please don't let us die—

But porch beams crumpled in around them before she could finish the prayer.

TWENTY

"Olivia? Olivia!" Daniel scrambled over the broken pile of timber that had been his front porch, searching the wreckage. He couldn't see Olivia anywhere. "Shout if you can hear me!"

Oh, Lord, where is she? Was she buried underneath all this? Is she even still alive?

There was a groan to his left. He turned. Jesse was trapped under a support beam.

Daniel picked his way over quickly and checked Jesse's pulse. It was strong, and there was no visible head trauma. Daniel grabbed Jesse's hands and duct-taped them together.

His eyes snapped open. "You're dead. You're both dead. When I catch you and that—"

He slapped a piece of duct tape over Jesse's mouth.

Then he saw her. Olivia was lying deep inside a pile of crumbled wood. He ran toward her. Her eyes were closed. Her face was pale. *Lord, please let her be okay.* He knelt down and gently pulled her body out of the wreckage. He cradled her into his chest. His eyes brushed the side of her face. "Olivia? Honey? Can you hear me?"

Green eyes fluttered open. He'd never seen anything more beautiful in his entire life.

"Hey!" A smile crossed her lips but her voice was faint. "That was some plan."

"Yeah." He chuckled softly. "Are you okay?"

"I think so." She took his hand and tried to pull herself to her feet. A cry escaped her lips. She fell back onto the wood. "I hurt my ankle."

"Hopefully it's not broken, just sprained." He slid his arms under her limbs and picked her up. He carried her through the rubble and out into the trees. "We'll get you to the car and to a hospital."

Her hands slid around his neck. Her heart beat into his chest. "Where's Jesse?"

"Trapped well enough that he can't chase us. But alive. Looks as though Jesse and the Faceless Crew will all live to face justice."

Branches pressed up against their bodies. Her arms tightened their grip on his neck. "When you said you had a plan, I was expecting something a little more complicated than jumping out a window and dropping a roof on top of him."

"Well, we didn't have that many options." He chuckled softly. "You're the one who taught me it was sometimes good to be impulsive."

Dazzling blue spread across the sky above them. The world was silent except for the sound of his feet moving through the underbrush and her breath against his neck.

"So now what?" she asked.

"Now we drive to Barrie. Trent lent me a disposable cell phone. As we go, you can keep trying your sister. She'll be so thrilled to hear your voice. Then the cops will come to arrest Jesse, Shorty and Brute. We'll provide the authorities with some really good information. You'll end up with a pretty major story." He bent closer to her. "And I'll ask you out for dinner. Somewhere you and I can sit alone, with quiet and candlelight, without anyone shooting at us and nothing exploding."

"Dinner?" Her breath teased his skin. "Last I heard, you just wanted to grab a quick coffee." Her lips brushed against his jaw, sending a shiver down his spine, then up into his heart.

He pulled her tighter into his chest. "Let's just say I've realized I want to get to know you better."

Then, before another word could escape her mouth, he brought his mouth down toward her, and their lips met in a kiss.

EPILOGUE

Spring sunlight streamed through the picture windows and spilled out onto the living room floor where Olivia knelt spreading *Torchlight News* page proofs all over Daniel's freshly installed hardwood floor.

His Olivia. His bride.

It had been six and a half months since their whirlwind romance had led to marriage. So many times, in what now felt like the distant past, he'd told himself he'd never trust his heart to another fast-burning romance. But now, as he woke up every morning amazed to find her there, asleep against his chest, he knew he'd never felt happier.

Daniel stood in the kitchen doorway and watched her for a moment as she shuffled the papers out across the floor and back again. Less than a day after the Faceless Crew had found justice, Vince had driven all the way up to the Barrie hospital to visit the two recuperating members of his battle-weary staff.

Olivia was shocked when Vince had told her the real reason he hadn't seen her in the writing pool was he wanted her as a key member of his administration team, but Daniel hadn't been surprised for a moment.

Olivia wasn't just good at one thing. She was like a firefly, shining in a million different places at once.

"You going to come in or you just going to stand there?"

He chuckled. "You looked busy, Madame Editor."

"I'm always busy, and you should see the photos Ricky's sent me for the cover. They're spectacular." She glanced up and grinned. Soft red hair fell around her face. Bright eyes looked up into his, filled with far more love than he'd ever thought he'd deserved to find. "Also, I'm only an assistant editor now. Don't have me taking over Vince's job too soon. I'm just barely managing to juggle the number of tasks and responsibilities I have as it is."

"The job suits you perfectly. Anything less than constant chaos and you'd get bored."

Her eyes twinkled. "Maybe."

Yeah, Vince had known exactly what he was doing when he'd made her his second-in-command. He'd never met someone so capable of juggling everything at once.

"He says as long as I can email him next week's layout by tonight, I'm welcome to work from home tomorrow instead of driving in. Vince is really open to letting me split my time between here and the city." She slowly climbed up to her feet. "Did you manage to talk to Sarah?"

He shook his head. He'd driven in to visit her once a week since her arrest. She hadn't agreed to see him once, even when he'd sent her a gift for her eighteenth birthday, or when he'd written her a letter telling her that he and Olivia were getting married.

Last he'd heard, Sarah had stayed true to her childish threats and wasn't cooperating with the police investigation. Not surprisingly, neither of them had heard a word from Trent since giving their final statements. But Daniel's new sister-in-law, Chloe, had told them that Shorty had been quick to turn on the remains of the Faceless Crew, Sarah and Jesse. She seemed confident their trial would end in a guilty verdict and justice for everyone involved.

"Not yet, and apparently she's fired yet another lawyer." Which was no longer his concern now that the eighteen-year-old had control over her inheritance. Not that it would do her much good behind bars. "I'll keep trying."

"I know you will. I love that about you. I've never met anyone as steadfast as you." She crossed the floor toward him. His arms spread apart to make room for her as her hands slid around his waist. "I know you said we were finally going to be rebuilding the porch this weekend. But I think we should really start on the second floor. There's only so long you can expect me to live on just a main floor."

His lips brushed across her forehead. "We have a plan—"

"I know. You taped it to the kitchen wall and color-coded it and everything—"

"It involved my first finishing the living room, erecting a temporary tent garage and converting my office into a master bedroom before we got married."

"Which you did." Her lips brushed his neck. "Which was a huge amount of work considering you proposed on our third date and we got married four months later."

"Which was quite enough to tackle before the worst of the winter hit. I'm exhausted."

"I know." Her mouth brushed against his ear. Her lips travelled up his jawline.

She was teasing him and he couldn't figure out why.

"Then we're agreed that we're building a new garage and porch this summer." He pushed her back and held her there with his hands on her waist. "Your home will have a lovely new second floor in two years' time."

She took her hands in his and slid them over her stomach. "I'll give you nine months. Well, eight months and a bit." Tears of joy filled her eyes and lit up every corner of his heart. "We're having…" Her voice caught in her throat.

He pulled her into him and wrapped his arms around her.

"A baby?" He whispered the word. A baby? A child of his own. *Oh, Lord, but I'd given up on that dream so many years ago.* "We're having a baby? But I'm turning forty in less than two years, the house is nowhere near finished, I'm still doing contract work, we were talking about my going back into private security and you've started a new job and—"

"We're going to have to make a whole new plan." She laughed through the tears.

"Yeah, guess we will." He pulled her tighter. "And I can think of no one else I'd rather have beside me."

Then his lips found hers again, and he kissed the woman he loved as a deeper, stronger joy than he ever expected to feel filled his core.

* * * * *

Dear Reader,

I'm so glad you decided to pick up this book and share Olivia and Daniel's story with me.

Like Olivia, I started my writing career as a journalist, working mostly for small independent papers like *Torchlight News*. Looking back on those fun and busy times, I'm very grateful for the journalists and editors who mentored me and helped me improve as a writer. While I never chased off after a murderer, there were several times when I, too, needed an editor to come along and remind me to balance my enthusiasm and energy with some good old-fashioned patience and planning.

After telling Luke's and Jack's stories in *Silent Hunter* and *Deadline*, I got to thinking about how their happily-ever-afters might have impacted the colleagues they left behind. My former coworkers are now spread around the world having families and adventures of their own. I'm excited for them and I miss them sometimes, too.

Like Olivia and Daniel, I hope you'll find the strength, joy and faith for whatever changes and new adventures you face.

Thank you for sharing the journey with me,

Maggie

REQUEST YOUR FREE BOOKS!

2 FREE RIVETING INSPIRATIONAL NOVELS
PLUS 2 FREE MYSTERY GIFTS

RIVETING INSPIRATIONAL ROMANCE

YES! Please send me 2 FREE Love Inspired® Suspense novels and my 2 FREE mystery gifts (gifts are worth about $10). After receiving them, if I don't wish to receive any more books, I can return the shipping statement marked "cancel." If I don't cancel, I will receive 4 brand-new novels every month and be billed just $4.99 per book in the U.S. or $5.49 per book in Canada. That's a savings of at least 17% off the cover price. It's quite a bargain! Shipping and handling is just 50¢ per book in the U.S. and 75¢ per book in Canada.* I understand that accepting the 2 free books and gifts places me under no obligation to buy anything. I can always return a shipment and cancel at any time. Even if I never buy another book, the two free books and gifts are mine to keep forever.

123/323 IDN GH5Z

Name   (PLEASE PRINT)

Address   Apt. #

City   State/Prov.   Zip/Postal Code

Signature (if under 18, a parent or guardian must sign)

Mail to the **Reader Service:**
IN U.S.A.: P.O. Box 1867, Buffalo, NY 14240-1867
IN CANADA: P.O. Box 609, Fort Erie, Ontario L2A 5X3

**Are you a current subscriber to Love Inspired® Suspense books
and want to receive the larger-print edition?
Call 1-800-873-8635 or visit www.ReaderService.com.**

* Terms and prices subject to change without notice. Prices do not include applicable taxes. Sales tax applicable in N.Y. Canadian residents will be charged applicable taxes. Offer not valid in Quebec. This offer is limited to one order per household. Not valid for current subscribers to Love Inspired Suspense books. All orders subject to credit approval. Credit or debit balances in a customer's account(s) may be offset by any other outstanding balance owed by or to the customer. Please allow 4 to 6 weeks for delivery. Offer available while quantities last.

Your Privacy—The Reader Service is committed to protecting your privacy. Our Privacy Policy is available online at www.ReaderService.com or upon request from the Reader Service.
We make a portion of our mailing list available to reputable third parties that offer products we believe may interest you. If you prefer that we not exchange your name with third parties, or if you wish to clarify or modify your communication preferences, please visit us at www.ReaderService.com/consumerschoice or write to us at Reader Service Preference Service, P.O. Box 9062, Buffalo, NY 14240-9062. Include your complete name and address.

LIS15

Love the Love Inspired
book you just read?

Your opinion matters.

**Review this book on your favorite
book site, review site, blog or your own
social media properties and share your
opinion with other readers!**